THE

VANISHED

© Marissa D'Angelo

BOOKS BY MARISSA D'ANGELO

THE

VANISHED

DEDICATION

THIS BOOK IS DEDICATED TO THE WISHES THAT
YOU NEVER THOUGHT WOULD COME TRUE IN
YOUR WILDEST DREAMS.

PREFACE

Many years ago, people sacrificed livestock that they used to feast on for the gods above, believing it would bring them luck and fortune. For many, this seemingly worked. For others, misfortune still swarmed their daily lives like a disease. Through the generations, people ceased to believe in such gods and goddesses, but all that remained was the very thought of souls reigning down from above, controlling our destiny.

No one knows who controls our destiny and future, but it is evident that a higher power resides above us all. Looking over your shoulder to see if you're being watched and finding no one at all can be haunting. Whether it be something we do not understand, or our own kind, it is certain there *is* something out there

lurking in our shadows.

TRANCE

1

Gentle caresses of the harp opened up the altar to a mystical place. Each note served as a guide through a forest full of life and marrow. The simple melody grasped the spectator's hearts as they, too, traveled through this forest. With each careful step, I felt closer and closer to tranquility.

A soft stroke on the black and white keys seemed to have awakened the others. The notes enveloped the once singular melody in a blanket of suppression. As the soft tone of the harp shrank, other sounds filled the air. It was all too harmonious to ignore. With careful steps,

I walked past the various people that sat in each pew, beside one another. None of them looked the same, but instead as if they came from all different paths of life. Beggars who stayed street-side left their signs to follow their ears. Their ripped clothing and drawn complexion gave their hardships away almost immediately. Doctors who must have heard the symphony from their operating rooms were sucked into a trance and found themselves in this enchanting room beside the beggars. They hadn't even stopped to take their stethoscopes or lab coats off. Couples and families that had just come from a night out at a restaurant, must have dropped their utensils the instant they heard. As the waiters saw customers leaving by the dozens, they too wandered out into the night. Soon, there would barely be enough seats for people in the cathedral-like room.

Without a word or glance, people took their seats beside one another in various pews. There was a dim light in each corner, leaving the center dark and gloomy. An altar was completely filled with orchestra members who performed without stopping. Without a conductor, they played on as if they were programmed robots repeating and repeating their notes. I watched in awe at how focused they were, but felt a bitterness in my stomach for what would soon come.

Ancient murals and stained glass windows lined the walls in the endless room. A dark statue's broad wings stretched out toward the audience. The black hooded robe that covered most of its head left me in question at what lie underneath.

On the other side of the altar was another god-like statue, but it was white in contrast. It appeared to be much more human-like if not for its wings. This statue revealed much more, as its arms were toned with muscles. It was not standing upright. Instead, it was leaning down over a person who appeared to be asleep. From my college studies of Greek mythology, I had briefly remembered Hyriad's poem of Hypnos, along with his many siblings. Hypnos was the Greek god of sleep, and the fact he stood beside someone who had been sleeping meant it was likely he had that effect on them. Without a dark cloak like the other statue had, this one had a chiton covering his body…. The entirety of his torso and waist were covered, but the smooth satin gently fell from his shoulder, revealing his muscular shoulder. The only other time I had ever seen someone with such muscles was when I would watch the Hercules cartoon as a child. A trance glazed over the orchestra and audience.

If one statue was Hypnos, it was very likely the other was Thanatos, who resembled Death.

All too suddenly, I spotted a dark shadow as it drifted across the room and wandered toward the corner. Quietly standing up from my pew, I tiptoed by the people sitting near me. *What was lurking in the corners while the others sat there, oblivious and continuously amused by the melody?*

The sudden movements I made seemed to have no effect on those around me. No one took their eyes off the stage. I could've jumped up and down while flailing my arms about in each aisle, and they still wouldn't have noticed. They didn't even blink as they watched and listened. When I reached the corner of the room where I saw the shadow, I found nothing but the dim light. I looked around at the walls and floor and saw nothing. *What happened to it?*

I drew closer toward the exit, of which I didn't even remember walking in. Towering Victorian doors stood in between my grasp of freedom. Just a few steps away and I could leave behind whatever this place was. Breathing a sigh of relief, I clung to the handle and gave it the strongest pull I could, only to find it wouldn't open. I tried pushing the handle the other way. Eventually, I dismissed the idea of having to tip-toe around and, since the others barely noticed my presence, I threw my whole body into the door, hoping it would fling open. Upon doing this a few more times, I quickly realized we were all locked in.

"Can someone help me?" I asked urgently. With no response, I looked back at the audience, still in that strange trance. No one had turned or even flinched at my voice. The orchestra continued on and now, they were violently playing at a much faster tempo.

Just then, movement danced before my eyes as I tried to follow it. I rushed to get across to the diagonal corner of the room in time. I gazed at it for only a split second before my body became weak. The shadow. I rushed toward the other corner of the room. As soon as I reached it, it was still there. Only this time, I stood next to it for a split second and in the next, I could barely feel anything as my body went completely numb. At first, my legs felt like bags of sand as I tried to lift them to move. Gradually, the entirety of my being felt as though I was no longer in control. When I looked down at my feet, they were turning dark and lifeless. A shadow seemed to extend up from there, taking away any remaining sign of life from me. When the darkness spread up to my waist, I yelped, surprised my mouth could still move. No one answered as they stayed entranced in the melody that was still ongoing.

Before I knew it, my entire body was wrapped in the shadow. What felt even worse than no longer being in control of my body was the fact there was no one that would save me. Although the room was full to capacity, not one soul broke out of the music's grasp to come save me. No one could hear me. No one could help. I tried pushing myself to run away or find another way to escape, but it was too late. I was merely a shadow in the room. A lifeless shadow no one could see.

Though my eyes were wide open, I couldn't seem to blink. In the very corner of my eye, something was missing. Despite the people staying in their pews, the statues that towered over them were no longer there. Without being able to move, I was forced to look frantically around in the same spot over and over again. I hoped I was only seeing things or someone was playing a trick on me. The statues had been there...hadn't they? I remember walking by them and there wasn't the slightest bit of movement from either. As the music mirrored my heart in its racing beat, footsteps that I had almost mistaken for drums—although there were none on the altar—approached . When I looked back at the audience, they were no longer staring at the altar...but instead, their eyes were glued to me. A woman that sat beside her child in one of the front pews had glossy eyes, as if she somehow could still convey emotion despite being paralyzed. It appeared as though she was trying to fight whatever was causing the paralysis that immobilized her, along with everyone else in the room...even me. The footsteps I had once heard ceased along with the music and the entire room was no longer focused on the orchestra that had been playing continuously through all of this. Dark wings extended into my view; swiftly folding back as the hooded man crept before me. Somehow, the statue was no longer frozen in position as it had been. It was moving. It was real. I wasn't able to see his face since his hood remained over his head as he looked down at the ground. The coldness of his body matched his previously frozen state, but his movements were similar to that of a soldier...unbending and marching closer to me. He reached out his hand as if expecting me to take it willingly. Although I still couldn't feel my body, I saw my arm raise in the corner of my eye. I was no longer in control of what I was doing. He controlled me while I placed my hand atop his cold, pale fingers. With his other hand, he took mine and turned me around. I could no longer see what he was doing, and it raged me to no end. In the next second, I was no longer standing but instead, looking at the ground from over his shoulder. He had effortlessly draped me over his arm as if I were nothing other than a towel. I wanted to kick and scream...tear my nails into him...and break free. But I couldn't. As he continued to walk in front of the audience, I locked eyes with a man that held a violin under his chin. He seemed to be in a frozen state, too. But this man differed from the rest because I felt like I had seen him before. He was staring straight back at me with worry in his eyes, just as the woman had. Before I could gaze at him any longer, the dark-winged man turned and walked a few more steps before he reached a pew where he plumped me down on. Although I wasn't able to move my positioning, his cold hands grasped mine as he placed them on my lap and gently touched my chin to move it up, as if to watch the performance along with everyone else. While I had expected violence from this man, his fingertips felt more sensitive to the touch than anything I had felt before. The audience still looked as though they were in a trance before me, but their bodies were also dark and lifeless. We were all just shadows in the room; lost and forgotten.

As the dark-winged statue left, the other one with white wings, in contrast, peered out from the side of the pew. He looked expressionless, just as the other had. His movements were much slower and deliberate. He seemed different from the other statue in that he locked eyes with me while the other had avoided any eye contact. When he walked toward me, he pressed his cold hand to my forehead. Right before he seemed to have any effect on me, I could feel one salty tear trail down my cheek and onto my lips. I felt tranquility envelop me into a state of dormancy. It was then that I realized I was now cemented to this pew, along with everyone else in the room.

REALITY

2

My eyes felt sealed over. I squeezed them and felt the tears stream down my cheeks. A bright light seared through, causing me to squeeze them shut again. I pulled my comforter over my head, realizing I was back in my warm bed again, relishing in the warmth of the sheets. What I would do to stay here just a while longer. Perhaps I would even take the day. I tried thinking about what I had dreamt the night before, but could barely seem to comprehend it. Had I been watching a scary movie the night before? Not that I had remembered...

A soft paw peeked under the sheets and touched my forehead. It nearly caused me to jump, still on edge from the nightmare. When I lifted a corner of the blanket, I felt relieved to see Toulouse trying to greet me. *Where were you when I was trapped in my nightmare, Toulouse?*

He pushed his way under the blanket with me and nuzzled close in a furry ball of warmth. He was an orange cat with a little belly of white. His paws were like white socks that stopped short of his orange fur. His long whiskers always tickled me whenever he tried waking me up. It never failed to work and no matter how tired I was each morning, I couldn't stay mad at him. When I rubbed his forehead, his loud purrs filled the once silent room.

A symphony sounded from the other side of the bed. I scrambled to turn it off as fast as I could since it reminded me of the orchestra in my dream. Toulouse's purrs stopped almost immediately as I pushed around the blankets to find my phone. It had been under my pillow the entire time. I struggled to turn it the right way, still feeling like my fingers were waking up from the terrible dream.

"Toulouse! You let me sleep in!" I groaned. It was already 10:45 and I couldn't remember the last time I had slept this long. I was so very late for my interview! Shoving the covers away from me, I quickly slipped on a pair of yoga pants and a gray sweater. I paced around the room and frantically looked for my boots. The sheets were as if a tornado had come and thrown them around on the bed. My make-up remover wipes were still on the dresser by the mirror, but no boots.

"Meow," Toulouse innocently declared from beside the bed. Poking out from right next to him was one of my auburn riding boots. I scurried over and hopped on one leg as I shoved my foot in. Toulouse had already scampered away before I could thank him. When I tucked my pants in the boots, I threw on a dark olive shawl and glanced at myself in the mirror, shrugging. My dark red hair was a mess and there were bags under my eyes. The green in them almost made me look like I had been possessed. I might as well have been with the dream that I had. I pulled a white scrunchy out of the first drawer of my nightstand and pulled my hair back in a ponytail. There was no time for a shower and I had to get going to my first appointment. As a journalist, I would set up a series of interviews to investigate any crimes that were ongoing. Despite the chief's many warnings, I was solely focused on the string of disappearances that had plagued the town in recent months.

I looked over at the room adjacent to mine. The door had been closed for far too long, but I couldn't get myself to open it. Normally, I would say goodbye to my roommate, Izzy, but she was one of the many victims that just hadn't ever come back one day. Izzy worked for the same office that I did, but was out in the field less. She would look up the whereabouts of cell towers that suspects' phones would send pings off of so that the police could locate them and take them in. Other times, she would just be doing other research on the computer.

One night, we had planned to stay in and binge watch sappy movies while eating all the sweets we could without making ourselves sick and she had never shown. When I called her, she was just leaving work on a day I had off. I remember her voice sounding as though there was something wrong, but she was quick to reassure me she would be home within the hour. Before I could ask where she was, I heard the click and looked down at the black screen on my phone with hesitation. That was the last I had heard from her.

When I was just about to walk out the door, Toulouse ran over to me and rubbed his body up against my leg. I patted him a couple times on the head as his eyes were bulged in confusion from the sheets being thrown over him.

"I'm sorry, Toulouse! I've got to go to work. Thank you for finding my boots!" I screamed as I slammed the door shut and fumbled for my keys to lock the door.

I lived in a white townhouse that stood out from the light blue townhouses beside it. There was a little garden area in the front that had frozen dry from the winter, but still showed some remains of last year's flowers. The corpse of a giant sunflower leaned against the front window. The townhome wasn't a perfect place, but it was home for the time being. It was also very close to some forests I frequently visited and shops I explored from time to time.

At the start of college, I knew that something with writing would best suit me. There was teaching writing to students, creative writing, or screen writing. The first was much too overrated for me, as my mother was a teacher and never took a day of rest. The latter called for luck and funding, of which I had neither.

Throughout my time as a student, corruption became more and more apparent. Each day, it felt as though I was drowning in it. Whether it be from my classmates meeting up with professors for late night visits to try to "beg" for better grades, news reporters' robotic ways of skewing information left and right, and real stories being shushed and pushed to the side while attention was turned elsewhere to places that mattered, but not nearly as much as what was truly going on in the world.

That's when I found myself working as a journalist. I would frequently go to the police station so often that they had a desk for me there.

Mother attempted to talk me out of it, but it was no use. Once my mind was set, it was done. My weeks consisted of starting at the very bottom of the force and I was given the worst assignments no one else wanted. There were times I could've sworn the entire force had come up with a joke of an assignment for me to go on. One time, there was a "missing goat," that only I was able to investigate. They sent me to a farm, and the farmers seemed to go along with it. We eventually found that goat at another person's farm. How, you ask? An anonymous tip. I felt the whole thing was silly, and a setup. But who would honestly waste the time to do all that? My weekends were my time where I chose the stories I wanted to investigate. My main objective was to find out about the disappearances the news seemed to conveniently leave out of all of their reports.

I knew I had to keep this to myself because of my association with Izzy being a victim of the disappearances. So this interview was part of my side-gig where I planned to find out the root of all of this and maybe...hopefully, bring Izzy back someday. As I walked by her room, I was tempted to go inside to reminisce when we moved in together and all the bad dates she or I had that we would eat tubs of ice cream afterwards to cope. The first few weeks that she was gone, I could barely even get myself out of bed. It was hard to be alone. But as soon as the idea came into my mind that she could still be out there somewhere and I could bring her back, waking up became that much easier.

Although it was Saturday, I had an appointment to meet with a potential witness of a disappearance that had occurred most recently. When I finally managed to get ready and leave the house, I went to a local coffee shop. In the front windows, a man was sitting alone with his head down. He wore a golfer's hat, except it was backwards. Since his back was toward me, I couldn't quite make out what he looked like. It appeared as though he had ordered a water, which was strange as most would've requested a coffee. There were not very many people inside. I grabbed my journal and pen, then quickly rushed in.

INTERVIEW

3

"Hey there, Jerome?" I hesitated for a moment. He stood up and pulled out my chair, waiting for me to sit in the spot he had chosen. It was a little strange because, instead of sitting across from one another as people normally do, I sat beside him while looking at the wall before us.

I followed his cue and waited for him to take his seat next to me. He was an undercover cop that had tried to follow the same investigation I was currently on, but seemed to have given up. From the previous conversation we had, he noticed disappearances from the plethora of phone calls coming in at the station. People often called him on his private phone just to reach out to find their lost family member. As soon as he tried to take it up at the station, he was shut down in an instant and told not to dig into the investigation ever again. Although they explained the disappearances to just be people moving out of town, it still didn't make sense why no one could get in touch with them.

That is when we met. I had just called him because it was my roommate who had been taken. He called me back after his talk with his boss and explained we had to meet in person. He wanted me to ask him any questions at all that I had about the disappearances as long as I kept his name out of the story.

We sat there in silence for a few moments. He looked like he hadn't shaved for at least a couple of days.

Stubble framed his face. His ocean blue eyes glanced over at me for a moment. The lightness clashed with the stubble that covered most of his face, softening him a bit more.

There was a very sad aura that surrounded him. He seemed emotionless. It was as if he wore a mask most times and revealed nothing to anyone at all. Even the slightest bit of sarcasm would jump right over him without so much as a smirk in return. I remembered him briefly from the station and he was one that kept to himself. Izzy would often joke that I had a crush on him, but I always felt like he was disinterested. When others at the station would have game nights or go out drinking, he'd always pass.

"Alice, I am ready when you are," he said in a solemn tone, taking a quick sip of his water. All business was understandable when it was taken in this context.

"Sure. In what alley was the most recent victim taken?" I asked as I opened to the next free page of my journal.

"Londerview Alley. It is right next to this coffee shop, actually. The only reason I know about it is because I had yet another person call me for help in finding their son, Jack, who had just come to buy a coffee here." He sighed and took yet another sip. Perhaps it was vodka in there... I wouldn't have been surprised at how this career often drove people to alcohol as a means of coping. Noticing I was still scrambling to write as fast as I could in cursive, he waited patiently.

"But we made plans to have coffee here before we even knew of this..." I said, trying to put the pieces together. "It all feels so coincidental now. We have come here to talk about the disappearances and yet another occurs less than a day before we come here."

"I don't know what to say...none of this makes sense to me either. I try to keep to myself so I don't get into much trouble and it always has a way of finding me, it seems..." His shoulders lifted up and back down as if to gesture to me he honestly had no idea. He continued when I didn't respond and I only nodded my head in understanding.

"When they expected Jack back from work that day, he never showed." He stopped right there and looked all around us as if to make sure no one was eavesdropping, then continued.

"They called his boss and found out he never arrived that day at work. So, they suspected his last appearance was here. He had a routine of getting his coffee here before heading off to work each day. I asked the shop owner if they had any details about this and they said he left to go on his way, but one worker noticed he took a right down the alley. They suspected he was possibly meeting up with a friend or something."

"So, how did you find out he had been in that alley?" I asked, probing for details.

He leaned back in the seat beside me and rested his hands behind his head as if to create a sort of pillow for himself. I was still writing notes from what he had just been saying, and he seemed to be giving me time to finish.

"Well, I went into the same alley he was supposedly last seen in and found his coffee set down on the ground. It had his name printed on it and not one drop was sipped. I privately ran it for any DNA traces or fingerprints and the only match was his own, so no other suspects are on the table at this time. This is pretty much the same story with all the missing persons.

"I keep telling these callers I will look into it, but know I will never be able to tell them what happened. I can't help but to feel as though it must be connected somehow to someone higher up or someone in the station. I know there is some connection somewhere or else they would not have shut down my investigation so abruptly and with no form of explanation."

As I was sloppily writing notes all over the pages within my journal, I could see Jerome put his head in his hands from the corner of my eye. This was a huge stressor for him. It sparked the thought of him possibly losing someone due to the unexplainable disappearances going on. He already knew about my roommate, but I was curious if he had known someone that was lost. I didn't want to ask, afraid of digging too deep when I had just barely scratched the surface.

"Anything else left at the scene?" I tried to think of other possible hints that could lead me to finding out more information on the missing person's whereabouts. I wished Izzy was still here so she could run phone records on him. That would definitely give some insight into who he had last spoken to.

"No...that was it. Well, actually, the coffee and his car keys were placed right next to each other. So, we don't know how he made it out of there without a car.

And we figured he couldn't have made it very far on foot. That's why my thoughts are on some sort of abduction."

Well, that key info was almost left out... Glad I asked. There were too many underlying questions I still had. If he was abducted, why had no one seen him leave with someone else? And an abduction would have most likely involved some sort of struggle to break free on the victim's part. There was only one way out of that alley and that was past the coffee shop. Surely, someone from here must have seen him come back out. But Jerome had asked. The shopkeepers and workers only saw him go in, but not come out. Was there any connection between the people who were abducted?

"Would you say any of the abductees had anything in common at all? Age, hangouts, friends, anything?" I asked in hope of some ground-breaking response.

My question was met with a deep sigh. "I thought of that too and tried all avenues. There really was nothing at all connecting any of the people. Differing sexes, races, schools, ages, religions, families... As far as I know, these people may have gone to the same mall in town, but not much—"

My pen dropped from the sweaty grasp that just held it. The excessive note-taking had ceased when Jerome's body grew tense. What he felt transferred to me somehow, since I felt it too. I followed his gaze and found him looking intently out the window. From the window's reflection, a figure that looked as though it was the chief of police drifted through the door of the shop. I glanced back to confirm it was, in fact, the chief at the station. His dark brown hair was short and graying on the sides of his head while he wore a hat to cover the balding in the very middle of his head. Only a few of us were lucky enough to see the embarrassing sight that lay beneath the hat. His face was permanently a shade of light red after years of high blood pressure and, likely, cholesterol damaged his body. The buttoned-down shirt he wore was half tucked into his pants. If he was here today, it meant he was working at the station. It was a Saturday, and he usually took the day off, but lately had been working more. Occasionally, he would send one of the other officers to fetch breakfast donuts and coffee, but this time it seemed he must have wanted an excuse to get out of the office for longer. I wondered if it had anything to do with the mystery Jerome and I had just been talking about.

He was a boss to both of us and would surely know what we were up to if he caught us together. The station thought they could use a journalist to write up stories for them if needed; I took the job as soon as I knew it was available. I now realized exactly why he chose to sit here. He must have felt as though he was being watched or followed. He slipped a note onto the seat of the chair he had just been sitting on and got up in a hurry.

Through the reflection, I could see our boss had not quite noticed we were even there. His loud voice blared through the coffee shop as he was busy ordering donuts and coffee for the station. Workers behind the counter rushed around to keep up with his order. One man went toward the donuts with a huge tray to place them in while another prepared coffee cups, marking each one with initials for some complicated coffee mixture.

On the other side of the shop, Jerome took his coat and left in an instant. All that remained of him was the note he left on the seat.

CONTINUANCE

4

Although Jerome was long gone, I stayed at the shop for a while longer to ask some shopkeepers additional questions he may not have asked. Not saying he wasn't an outstanding detective, but, hey, you never know and it certainly couldn't hurt to try.

"Hey...Monica?" I eyed the waitress' name tag. She was around my age, mid 20s I could guess, and average height. Her dirty-blonde hair was swept back in a ponytail. Smart. I'd rather not have hair in my food and I'm sure no one else would want that either. She wore thick-rimmed glasses, which puzzled me when she could just get contacts and not have to worry about her glasses fogging up whenever she was around a hot plate of food. Her black blouse was tucked into dark dress pants, which was a typical look for a waitress. One of my first jobs was as a waitress and I remember having to go out to buy a whole new wardrobe just to match their criteria of black shirt, black pants. I winced, just thinking about how I'd have to deal with angry customers from time to time. In the restaurant business, you would often find people's worst sides coming out.

She was just walking toward the back when I had stopped her. Monica instantly concealed what had been a frown with a forced smile.

"Hi there. Do you need to be seated?" she asked, clearly in work-mode.

"No, thank you. I just wanted to ask you a few questions, if you have a minute? It will be quick," I responded, hoping she wouldn't shut me down right away.

She looked as if she was going to deny my request, but then glanced at the many empty seats around the restaurant. The chief was just walking out with a tray of donuts for everyone back at the station. It looked like their biggest order was just about done. She bit her lip and looked back at me.

"I suppose I have a minute. What would you like to know?"

I pulled out my notepad in an instant. It felt as though it was attached to my hip most days, since I rarely went anywhere without it. I never knew if or when I was going to find another story to write about.

"Do you remember the man who came here, who vanished in the alley nearby?"

She nodded.

"How did he act right before he left? Was he in a rush...happy, down about something...?" I tried digging for any minor detail that could help.

She shook her head. I waited a moment to give her a chance to think. The waitress nervously scratched her head as if she were debating whether to reveal what she knew. Finally, after a few moments of an awkward silence, she decided to say something.

"Well, he did seem a little nervous. He was looking all around himself as if he was being watched," she said. I wrote BEING WATCHED in all capitals. She seemed to be looking at what I was writing and continued on. "I just can't think of who would be watching him, though.

But come to think of it...he was acting a little bit strange that day."

The vague answers weren't helping because they only left me with more questions to ask. It was better than nothing, though. I looked around the shop to make sure no one was listening to us. When it was still empty, I asked a lingering question I had.

"Was he acting as if he were hypnotized?" I asked, thinking of my ridiculous dream the night before. If there was no evidence of a struggle like he had been abducted and there was no reason for him to want to run away from his life, then perhaps he was in a trance of some sort. That was the only thing that made sense.

She squinted her eyes and looked out the window, trying to make just as much sense of all this as I was.

"It doesn't make sense…but yes. Jack comes into the coffee shop all the time and we have conversations about our lives as I'm getting his coffee. But that one morning, it was as if he was a total stranger when he came in. He didn't seem to recognize me and had this blank stare. He barely remembered what he even wanted to order, and I had to ask if he wanted his regular, which he, of course, said yes to. Then he took his drink in utter silence and walked out the door without even saying goodbye."

"And you didn't think to ask him if something was wrong?" I asked, not trying to blame her but wishing there was more to this conversation that she recalled.

"I would have, but we suddenly got slammed in the shop and everyone was either calling in or coming through the door."

"So then you didn't even see if he walked back out to his car, did you?"

At this, she hesitated and her lip quivered with her response as if it was a sudden realization on her part as well. "No, I did not..."

"Is it okay with you if I go out to that alley to check out the scene where he left his coffee?" I asked.

"They've checked that area again and again. I don't think you will find anything, but go right ahead." Monica breathed a sigh of relief, as if she were thankful I was finally going to stop with my interrogation.

"Hey..." I gently touched her arm when she was about to walk away. She turned and raised her eyebrows as if to ask what more I could possibly want. "Thank you. This really means a lot to me, especially since I think it could connect to my roommate's disappearance. If you can think of anything else, take my card and feel free to message me, day or night.. Sometimes we can't think of all the answers we need on the spot. My line is open," I offered. She took my card and gave another forced smile, walking behind the counter to straighten up the area.

My mind felt like it was going in circles. Just when I was starting to understand what was going on, a new curveball came around and struck me when I least expected it. I wished I could speak to Jerome again and ask him more, hoping he would add more clarity to the disappearances. My dream last night led me to believe I was now forming my own imaginary conclusions about what could have been happening. But the fact that Monica felt like he was in a trance too, meant that parts of my dream could have been true. I wondered if

Jack had been slipped a drug that caused him to act as if he was in a trance-like state. Before leaving, I ordered a hot chocolate and wandered outside into the brisk fall afternoon. I clung to the drink for warmth and zipped up my jacket, hoping I would magically grow warm once again.

When I walked beside the coffee shop, I imagined this may have been the same path Jack had taken during his last few moments. The bricks that lined the coffee shop mirrored the building on the other side, which was an old church. Jerome had said the only thing that was left of Jack was his coffee cup, sitting perfectly on the ground. In any other abduction, the victim would have likely struggled and the coffee cup would've been thrown at some point or other. There was only one option, which I wrote in my journal, using the brick wall as a temporary writing stand.

Suspect: Someone He Knew

I decided I would have to, somehow, compile a list of all the people Jack knew and cross off ones that had an alibi. I smiled down at my notebook, happy I now had some direction for my case. Taking one last look down the alley, I walked down a little farther, as if something would just fall from the sky to give me even more evidence. I pressed my hands against the brick, wondering how there wasn't more of a struggle. And if he went with someone he knew, why not bring his coffee? People claimed to have seen him go into this alley, but no one saw him come out.

Peering down at the empty ground, there wasn't even a trace of the coffee he had left. No stain, spill or anything. At the very edge of the alley, there was something black that stood out to me against the red brick. I slowly crept toward it. A breeze drifted into the alley and the small black object was gently lifted with the wind, only to fall back down again. I stopped where I stood so I could watch it. It was as weightless as a feather but appeared to be much longer than any feather I had seen before. I looked behind me and saw no one was there. When I continued on, I picked up the feather in my hands and noticed it was as long as my arm.

My mind instantly flashed to the dream I had and in the next moment, everything I had known no longer made sense. I felt for the crumpled-up paper in my pocket and unfolded it to find a short note left from Jerome. As soon as I read it, I couldn't help but shudder.

Do not trust anyone at the station.

CONSTANT

5

Consistency was what we held on to most in life. If not for a dose of familiarity, one wouldn't feel like they were truly home or able to recognize the world. What would be even more frightening was no longer having it in your life. At that point, it felt as if there was no home for you. When there was a dark time in my life, I tried to go to the place I had always known.

"Mom, Dad, are you guys in there?" I knocked on the door several times. I could hear the surround system blare through the house as if there was an earthquake shaking it. Dad loved going to the movies and got his own little movie theater installed in the house. But ever since then, they could barely hear anyone at the door over it. I walked around the back and the spotlight gleamed down on me as it sensed me walking past. As soon as I got there, I could hear Dad was watching Batman for what must have been the millionth time.

I brought out my phone and dialed his number. When he answered, I could hear his echo from inside.

"Hey Alice. How's your day off going?"

"Oh, just fine. You're watching Batman again, aren't you?" I asked.

"How do you know that?" He sounded skeptical, but I couldn't help but smile.

"I'm right outside, Dad," I finally said.

"What? Why didn't you knock?!" I could hear his phone fall onto the couch as he must've jumped up and walked to the back door to let me in. When he opened it, he hugged me, acting as if he hadn't seen me in a decade, even though it had only been a few days.

"Dad, you're squeezing me," I groaned.

"Well, I wouldn't have to if you gave me a better hug," he joked.

"I've got to talk to you about something concerning work."

"Is it that guy again that won't stop giving you looks at the station? I can have a few words with him…" Dad recalled something that I probably should have never even told him because, being the protective dad that he was, he would blow anything out of proportion.

"No, no, no...he's not a worry, forget about him."
Dad used to be a bodybuilder and also retired military.
To strangers, he was one of the most intimidating
people. But to me, he was always just like a big teddy
bear who had a heart made of gold. Whenever he left
the house, he would wear a hat but otherwise liked to
dress as comfortable as possible. Although he no longer
worked out much, he somehow managed to keep his
incredibly strong arms. At least I knew whenever I went
anywhere with him, no one would bother us.

"Is that Alice? Tell her to come eat. I've got some
breaded chicken that's almost done," Mom called out
from the kitchen. It was funny because my family would
always try to take care of you with food. Even if you
weren't hungry, as long as you were a guest in their

house...they would feel obligated to at least offer you some food.

As soon as I walked in the kitchen, I could see Mom flipping over chicken while they fried in oil. She heard me coming in and gave me a smile, looking back at the stovetop. She had red hair like mine and freckles to match. But she had blue eyes while I had Dad's brown eyes. He was Italian while she was Irish, which was not a match made in heaven in the least bit. I didn't really know how they got together because it never made sense since they were complete opposites.

"Alice told me that something happened at work," Dad said, in case she didn't hear.

"Is it that same guy?" I rolled my eyes and Dad just laughed. "What? Ok, one of you help me with these dishes."

I walked over and took a stack of three plates over to the table to set them down. Dad gathered the forks and knives.

"There's something strange happening," I said.

"You can say that again," Mom replied. I must've made a face that said it all because Dad burst out laughing even more.

"Come on, I'm serious..." I sat down and stabbed a piece of chicken with all my might. Mom recoiled as if it scared her, but Dad didn't seem to notice since he was scooping piles of mashed potatoes onto his plate.

"Alright, what's going on?" Mom asked.

"You know how I have been having those dreams? The ones where people just keep disappearing?" They both leaned in closer and waited for me to continue. I finished chewing the last piece of chicken I had cut and went on. "There have been so many disappearances the station seems to just be overlooking. There's Izzy, another guy by a coffee shop, and several more. I feel like they are connected."

"What makes you think that?" Mom asked. Dad scooped some more mashed potatoes onto my plate without me even having to ask. I took a spoonful and knew I had to stop myself because I could just keep snacking on them endlessly, especially with how Mom made them.

"Okay so...Izzy disappeared and everything was left just the way it was with her phone left behind. The last place she was seen didn't show any signs of a struggle... Then this guy, Jack, he was getting a coffee and the next thing everyone knew...his coffee cup was found sitting in the alley outside the shop."

"You don't really know the full story, though. Both people could have been involved in something you may never know about," Dad said, definitely recalling some of the investigation discovery shows he frequently watches.

"That's what I'm trying to find out. What were they both involved in? How are they connected?" I asked.

"You're probably dreaming about it because it has been bothering you. That's all," Mom said. I wondered whether or not I should tell her more about what else happened in the dream.

"Ok...how do you explain this? I had a dream of a man with black wings and he seemed to be from another world. Then, at the crime scene, I found a black feather." Saying it out loud made it feel that much more real.

"You're watching too many scary movies, and there are birds in the sky that could have dropped a few feathers. It's just a coincidence." Mom quickly shrugged off what I said. I looked over at Dad.

"I always think dreams are our subconscious telling us something. If you think it is your gut trying to tell you that there is some person out there taking these people, then you could be right," he admitted.

"It couldn't have been a bird. The black feather was way too long. If it were a bird, then it was from another time." I looked over at Mom.

"What did you do with it?" she asked.

"It's right in my car. I'll go get it and show you guys."

In the next moment, I left my plate exactly where it was and rushed outside, eager to prove my theory even though it was incomplete and I had no idea what would even come of it. I was just desperate to get someone—

anyone—on my side.

FEATHER

6

The night sky enveloped everything around me in pitch black. Unlike the city I lived in, there weren't any streetlights other than the motion detectors directly outside the house. A chilling breeze whistled through the air and sent chills down my spine. I pulled my jacket closer to me as I headed down my parents' driveway. When I reached my car, the motion detector lights shut off, and I fumbled for my keys in an attempt to turn some sort of light on so I could at least see again. After feeling for the metal keys in my pocket, I finally found them and pressed the button to unlock it twice.

Headlights flashed and reflected off the white garage door my car was just a few feet behind.

Some leftover bags from donuts I got were at the feet of the front passenger seat, which no one could sit in because of the extra jacket and backpack placed atop it. I brought my backpack everywhere, as if I were a school-aged child again. It was so much easier to always have everything you needed, even if you were on the go constantly. My interview notebooks, several pens, a planner, and a diary were my lifeline. The one thing I just couldn't live without was my planner above all the other things in there. Using a paper planner had a different feel to it because of how it felt to write each thing down and be able to bring it out and look at the entire month and not have to squint. Although, that's the very reason I *had* glasses…despite the fact I barely used them.

I opened up the back door so I could get the long black feather. Unknowing who could've been peeking in my car at the coffee shop, I had covered it with a blanket I also always kept in my car. When I pulled it back, the leather seats were the only things I found. I moved the blanket aside and rummaged through everything in the backseat. The feather was nowhere to be found. It had been my one piece of evidence that could've explained a lot, and now I looked like a complete fool because I had compared it to the dream I had. After moving almost everything in my car as if I was a tornado that had suddenly struck through the contents, I still wasn't able to find it. I slumped down in the backseat and closed the door, allowing the lights to dim from within. Staring out at the dark in silence, I felt both overwhelmed and defeated. But then it occurred to me someone had to have broken into my car in order to get the feather. Everything else was left exactly as it had been and even the blanket was placed so carefully to make it seem like it still concealed my one piece of evidence.

I didn't want to leave the car, afraid of what awaited out there for me. Part of me felt silly for being so paranoid, but also had every reason to believe that I wasn't safe...especially when something was stolen from me. That would have meant the person had been watching me all along. They would've known I went into that alley where I found the feather. And they would've also possibly followed me to my parents'.

Whoever they were, they could very well be just a few feet away for all I knew.

I grabbed my phone and longed to dial my dad so he could turn all the lights on and bring a flashlight out to come find me. But that would mean putting him in danger too, and I couldn't do that. Was I stupid for trying to solve this case on my own, especially when everyone at the station had warned me not to?

I decided to text someone else entirely. Someone I thought I would never contact again, especially since he seemed to not want us to be seen together in hopes we wouldn't be caught in pursuit of the unsolved cases. But he was the only one who who was on the same page as me.

Alice: Jerome, are you up?

A few minutes went by and I stared at the phone, urging him to answer as soon as possible.

Jerome: Yeah, what's up?

I didn't know where to start and wasn't sure a phone call could be trusted, so I just said the least amount that I could in the text.

Alice: Come to my place if you can. It's an emergency; I need to talk to you.

He answered much quicker on the next go-around and I was thankful for it. He must have been surprised to see my name pop up on his phone to begin with.

Jerome: Be there in 20.

I clicked the side of my phone and started my car, making sure several times that the doors were locked even though I knew I had already checked. From the car's digital screen, I was able to dial Mom's number. She answered almost immediately.

"Where are you going?" she asked, likely realizing since I never came back, I was leaving instead.

"I'm just going home," I said. I couldn't tell her I was meeting Jerome because they would have both been against it. He was a guy, and they didn't trust anyone to be alone with me in my apartment. Jerome worked at the station though, for longer than I did and this was something I had to talk with him about or I wouldn't be able to sleep tonight.

"Why? Where's that feather?"

"I'll show you guys tomorrow or something. I'll come by after work, okay?" It seemed she handed Dad the phone, or he took it from her because he was the next voice I heard.

"You better be here! We were waiting for you. I even paused Batman so we could finish it together," he said. The reminder of what we used to always do made me smile despite the current situation I was in.

"I'm looking forward to it. I love you," I said, wishing I could just have stayed in their house and slept over the night. But my mind always had to wander; especially when it was told not to go to certain places…that only made me all the more curious.

"I love you too! Goodnight. Text us when you get home," he quickly said, then hung up.

The drive back took around twenty minutes and when I was just a few minutes away from my townhome, my phone sounded with a text. I had it read aloud to me since I was driving.

"Jerome said, 'I'm here,' what do you want to say back?" The car's robotic voice read the message.

"Nothing," I said.

"You said, 'Nothing,' is that right?"

"No! Nothing!," I yelled.

"You said, 'No! Nothing!' Is that right?" It mocked me and I just ignored it at that point, aggravated. A dark challenger was in the driveway and at first, I felt skeptical but breathed a sigh of relief when I saw Jerome as he got out of the car. He gave me a wave and crossed his arms upon walking toward where I was parking. As soon as I pulled in, he helped me open my car door and had a worried look on his face, as if he had lost his best friend.

TRUTH

7

Toulouse must have scampered underneath the couch because when we walked in, he wasn't there. When there were new people in the house, he got very shy. I hadn't had anyone over since before Izzy disappeared. After Jerome finished asking me if I was okay ten or fifteen times, he finally sat down on the couch. His shoulders were still tense even as he just sat there.

"What happened?" he finally asked.

"I think someone is following me," I answered, still standing next to the door, unmoving from where I had just come in.

"Why?"

"Ever since I have been looking into the case, there's been strange things happening. I can't even explain them. I don't know how to say it because I feel you may think I am losing my mind." I looked down at my feet, avoiding any eye contact with him.

"Say it." He stood up and walked toward me. When he took my hand in his, a shock jolted through my body as if I had just been slightly electrocuted. I jumped away while he stood there, dumbfounded. "Sorry." I couldn't help but look straight into his eyes, still feeling the remnants of the shock he gave me. For some reason, I could trust him, even though I didn't fully know him.

"I have been having this dream about a man that resembles an angel except he has dark wings. Everything else is dark, too. I can't see him because he wears a black coat with a hood that covers his face...so I don't know who it is, but in the alley I found a long black feather that looked like it could have fallen off of one of his wings..."

"And?" he asked, eyebrows creased together as if he was having trouble believing anything I said. I didn't blame him.

"When I went to go get the feather that I thought would have served as some evidence of the disappearances, it was suddenly gone. I think whoever is involved in this case has been following me. They may have even been following you... I swear, it was in my car," I said and he didn't respond at first. He was clearly trying to make sense of what I just said, which is what I have been doing every second of the day. It was that, or he was plotting his grand escape from the crazed maniac, that I probably sounded like to him.

"Dreams are a part of our subconscious trying to tell us something. You've been on this case for a while and you lost somebody close to you. I think it's understandable," he finally said.

"But what does it mean?" I eagerly asked him.

"You think they are all connected and you're actively searching for any piece of evidence you can find."

"I just want to bring her back." I looked down and felt a tear stream down my cheek. Warmth spread across my face, and I knew I was probably bright red. In the dim light, I wasn't sure if he could see it as well, so I was thankful for that. In the next moment, I felt his hand as it gently grasped my wrist. This time, there was no shock. Only warmth in his touch. I looked up at his dazzling blue eyes.

"We're going to find her and figure it out, okay?" he assured me.

"But how?" I asked, grateful he wasn't taking advantage of the moment since the wall I normally put up came crashing down. For the first time in a while, I was completely exposed.

"Let's look at some of the other places where the people may have gone missing," he said. "Where were you in your dream?"

"I was in some kind of older church... I think it may have been the one near the coffee shop that Jack disappeared at."

"Then start there. But don't let anyone know what we're doing, okay?" He brought me in for a hug and it was the first one I had from a guy besides my dad in several years.

Just then, something fell off the coffee table by the couch. Jerome grew tense as he turned his body, shielding me from whatever was in the room. I couldn't see over him, but adjusted to the right so I could peek out like a scared child would hide behind their parent. After a few seconds of silence, Toulouse came right beside us and rubbed against my legs, then Jerome's. I was surprised because it was unlike him to show affection to a stranger. We both breathed a sigh of relief at the fact it was only Toulouse.

"Sorry, I should have probably mentioned I have a cat. I hope you're not allergic." I bit my lip.

"No, I'm not." Jerome crouched down to pet Toulouse. He was rubbing just under his chin and clearly knew the way to this kitty's heart. Toulouse lifted his head, allowing Jerome to pet him even more.

"Wow, he likes you," I said.

"Is that surprising?" he asked, looking up and winking. I never saw this playful side of Jerome before and I kind of liked it. Usually, he would be the quietest one at work; keeping to himself...in and out, right after his shifts.

"Well, I don't mean it like that. I mean, of course he likes you. What's there not to like? I mean—ugh." I wished I could have taken back my words and swallowed them, but they were already out in the open. I had meant to say Toulouse didn't usually like other people, but it somehow came out that way.

"Well, you're an ego boost, for sure. Maybe I should have spent time with you sooner," he laughed. I felt my cheeks grow red again.

"If that's what you think..." I joked. "Alright, thank you for meeting with me. I really do feel a lot better."

"Are you going to be okay?" he asked, clearly hesitant about leaving.

"Yes, I think so. I just got nervous about walking alone. I really felt like whoever was stalking me may claim me as their next victim in this... I guess I'm getting too paranoid." Reluctantly, I opened the door for him. He looked back at me just before he was about to leave. The glossy shine in his eyes reflected the moonlight.

"You have every right to be. If you need me, I'm just a call away. Okay?" he reassured me.

"Thank you. I really appreciate it," I said. "See you at the station tomorrow."

He waved and was off. As soon as I got into bed, I realized I hadn't called Dad and had a few missed calls from him. I called him back right away, worried that he had already gotten in his car to drive over so he could check on me. After several reassurances I was okay, he finally backed down and just told me to get some rest. I kept the hallway light on that night to not feel so alone.

DREAM

8

I found myself walking through the same alley that they had found Jack's lone coffee cup. All was quiet in the frigid night air, other than the thoughts that circled endlessly in my mind. There wasn't a hint of anyone else around, and the streets appeared to be empty of any life. The once bustling streets had turned into a ghost town as if a curfew had been put into effect. But why was I here? And better yet...how did I get here?

The struggle to stay warm crippled me as I searched for a place I could temporarily stay. Little by little, snowflakes trickled down onto me. With each touch, they melted instantly. I tucked my hands into my sleeves as much as I could since they were already beginning to turn a different color from the frigid air. Desperate, I ran into the building next door and quickly realized I was in an old, historic church. The intricate architecture gave off a glowing appearance from the slight bit of moonlight that crept through the ceiling window. I could feel my hands again as they thawed. As soon as I walked through the lobby of the church and passed the pews, goosebumps lined my skin and it wasn't because of the cold this time. Despite the perfectly warm church, it was déjà vu that now swarmed me in my thoughts and body alike.

This was the church I had dreamed of and never stepped foot in before this…if not for that dream I had. Unlike the nightmare that constantly echoed in my mind, the pews were bare with no orchestra in front of them. While I walked past each pew, there was one thing that laid open and out of place. The book of Genesis, that would have normally been closed and put away, laid open on the seat. It was strange to see this here since the pews usually kept Bibles, not Genesis by itself. I carefully crept beside it and sat down, taking the book in my hands to read it. It had been many years since I had last entered a church. When I was just a child, I went to Sunday school and received all of my sacraments. But as soon as I got to college, I no longer attended. I looked down at the passage and read it in my mind:

Now the serpent was more crafty than any other beast of the field that the Lord God had made. He said to the woman, "Did God actually say, 'You shall not eat of any tree in the garden?'" And the woman said to the serpent, "We may eat of the fruit of the trees in the garden, but God said, 'You shall not eat of the fruit of the tree that is in the midst of the garden, neither shall you touch it, lest you die.'" But the serpent said to the woman, "You will not surely die. For God knows that when you eat of it, your eyes will be opened, and you will be like God, knowing good and evil."

-Genesis 3:1-24

It was true. Although many people saw evil, they continued to follow it despite the warnings they were given. Even though some saw the good, they would turn and go a completely different direction. As people, we are all flawed in this way. And we have been flawed since the beginning of time.

A breeze whispered through the air and gave me goosebumps all over my skin. It sounded as if the door had just been pushed open and when I jumped to look back, it was slowly closing. There was no one next to it, though. I felt a strange presence somewhere in the room and looked around frantically. I crept over to the pew closest to me and crouched down, peeking slightly out into the main aisle. No one stood beside the door that had just been opened and the entire church seemed empty everywhere I looked. Could the wind have pushed the door so hard it opened? I guess it was possible. I was just about to get up when I saw the cloaked figure of someone beginning their descent down the aisle. As I quickly shoved myself back into the pew and crouched even further down to hide, the cloaked figure stopped right beside me. He didn't turn my way or look at me. Instead, he continued facing forward and seemed as if he was frozen in place. I looked up at him and felt my jaw drop at his towering black wings that protruded from his cloak. It was the same man from the dream I had the other night. Except...there was another. If this was Thanatos, then Hypnos was coming shortly after. Was this just another dream? I stared at him, knowing that he likely saw me, but for some reason wasn't pointing me out or anything like that.

"Stay quiet," he whispered without looking down. I peeked next to the pew and still saw no one, so figured he must be talking to me. I tried to further squish myself below the seats.

"Hello brother," the cloaked man said, continuing to stare in front of him.

"Are we going to gather the others again tonight?" A cold tone came from the other side of the church. I was just a few inches away from the cloaked man's waist, but he tapped his side a few times with his hand as if he was trying to tell me something. I couldn't quite figure out if and why he was hiding me.

"It is wrong," he replied.

"It is what we are intended to do...I lure them here in a trance while you take them. That's our purpose."

"We're planning the fates of others..."

"And?" The other man didn't seem to understand anything his brother was saying.

"Why don't we do this tomorrow night?" He pressed his smooth white hand against the edge of the pew I hid behind. There was a brief silence before his brother finally replied.

"I don't know what the difference is, but okay...tomorrow night it is." I could hear his voice as it came closer. Whoever this was, it was probably best they didn't see me. As soon as the man with the cloak began walking past my hiding spot, large black wings protruded out and nearly brushed into me upon his passing. He was walking toward his brother, almost as if to guide him away from my whereabouts. But why?

"Come. Let's go this way. I will be right back in a few moments, but I want to show you something, brother." He deterred him from coming near me.

"You're acting more strange than usual tonight... Are you feeling okay?" the one with the cold tone asked. When I felt like they were much farther away, I peeked out slightly from where I had been hiding to find they were the two men from my nightmare that night. The one with dark wings resembled Thanatos, and the other one with white wings was Hypnos.

"Eh, when don't I?" He laughed and their voices faded away until the church was as silent as it had been when I had first entered. I waited a few minutes and poked my head slightly above the pew. While the room had once warmed me to the point I could feel my fingers again, a draft breezed through, covering my skin in goosebumps once more. I had to get home. Somehow. I tiptoed down the aisle and toward the front of the church and nearly made it out of the door when

I saw something peculiar resting on the floor. Making sure no one had come from the other side of the church, I glanced back and was relieved they were still both off doing God knew what. The lighting was dim, so I couldn't tell what it was at first, but reached down and felt the cold metal key that someone had left. Footsteps approached and began making their way down the aisle. I quickly shoved the key into my pocket and ran out of the door into the piercing cold air. A thick blanket of black enveloped everything around me and it was then that I felt the most alone I had ever in my life.

DARK ANGEL

9

The slightest attempt at opening a door that was once thought to be permanently closed, could reveal endless possibilities. It was said when one door closed, another opened... but there is a never-ending amount of other doors one could take. The most fearful part of it all was the thought of what lay on the other side. Or who.

Walking into the unknown was one thing, but doing it alone caused ten times as much worry than anything else could. I had walked near the coffee shop before, but this time I had no car. There was no knowing how

I even got there or how I would get home. When I attempted to grab my phone, I realized my pockets were empty of everything but the key, which had sunk to the bottom. I couldn't even call a cab or friend to come pick me up. I was at least a mile away from where I lived, but it was bitterly cold. My fingers already felt numb in the few minutes I had been outside. As I tucked them in my sleeves, I was desperate to go back into the warmth the church had just provided me, even if it meant facing the two men I had only ever seen in my dreams. I couldn't even process what was going on and what they could've been up to, but my gut told me it was nothing good.

A few flakes of snow trickled down while I walked in the direction I thought was my home. Each time they touched the ground, they formed a white blanket on the ground I walked on. Behind me, a trail of my footprints gave way to anyone who wanted to follow me. I decided to try to throw them off and started walking to the right, then cut left quickly back into the alley beside the coffee shop. Bricks lined the building walls to my left and right, which led to a dead end. I turned and pressed my back against it, not knowing where to go next. It was the most peculiar thing... Luckily, no one had followed me into the alley... yet. The bricks I leaned against seemed different in some way. When I turned to look at them again, despite the darkness, I felt something was off. Pressing my hands along its coarse surface, there was a small hole the size of a pea in the center of one brick. I couldn't place why it was there or what it meant, but the frigid air served as a constant reminder I needed to get home before I froze to death. The dead end of the alley wasn't going to get me any closer if I just stayed there. I might as well have the same demise as Jack, who just seemed to disappear into thin air somehow.

A few streetlights flickered while the snow attempted to cover their entirety. A glow illuminated parts of the street and allowed me to see just a little despite the night. The night was bare of any existence other than my own as the wind swept the flakes of snow to and fro.

The snow that had blanketed the ground before me in a white embrace was bare of any footprints since I hadn't walked there before. Under one streetlight, I could see my own footprints behind me as the snow trickled in bit by bit to fill them in. If it was a crime scene, it could have covered up any of my tracks in the most perfect way so no one could find me. Once I reached the second streetlight, there was something off.

I knew I hadn't walked here before, but much larger footprints sank into the cold depths of the snow that was now piling up higher and higher. I stumbled in shock and felt my back press against something much smoother than the brick wall. I didn't want to turn around. I wanted to close my eyes and just wake up from whatever this was, but there I was almost frozen in place and next to someone I didn't dare turn around to see.

Dark black wings that matched the raven-colored night extended and folded in front of me as if it were a protective barrier. I could no longer see the light or anything else since it had concealed everything in its suppression. My fingers thawed, and I felt warm again almost instantly. When I turned, I couldn't see him, but knew he was there. He made no sound or gave the slightest hint of life, but I could feel him. The bare skin of his chest pressed against my cheek as he held me close to him. The wings that touched my back tickled me slightly.

"Why didn't you wait for me?" he asked and suddenly I remembered the church and how he had told his brother he would be right back. It would only make sense he planned to come for me after escorting his brother out. But why did he have to hide me from him?

"Who are you?" was all I could ask.

"Shhh."

The warmth of his chest pushed closer to my face as if he was shushing me by pressing himself into my lips. Although I still couldn't see anything from inside his dark wings, the snow being pushed down nearby alarmed me. As I wondered what it could be, I realized it was the sound of footsteps edging closer and closer. He reached into my pocket without warning and I felt the weight lift. He must have taken out the key I had found. The cold metal was in my hand the next instant. Before I could ask him why he was giving me the key and how he even knew about it, he was quick to whisper answers to my questions.

"Take this and run...run as fast as you can into the alley and you will find it," he whispered, then looked up. His wings extended, and I found light again from the dimly lit streetlights. Despite the long-lost light, the warmth was taken away too suddenly and caused me to hug myself. When I turned back, I could see the dark angel was still concealing where I stood as his wings were fully extended. Although I couldn't see his face, his back was now bare, which differed from the cloak he wore in the church. As the snow drifted down, each flake clung to his wings. They didn't stay there for long, gently dissolving shortly after they touched.

"Must you follow me wherever I go?" the dark angel asked. I couldn't see who stood on the other side of him, but I guessed it was his brother since they had just spoken in the church.

"You're hiding something, Thanatos," his brother said.

"And what am I hiding?" he asked, defensive. I heard the footsteps approach closer as Thanatos backed up an inch, clearly still trying to hide me.

"You tell me." I heard him move closer. "Why don't you fold in your wings again? It almost looks like there may be something....or someone behind you." His brother must have known him well.

"Run," Thanatos said under his breath, and I knew he wasn't speaking to his brother any longer. Instead, this was directed at me.

I ran back toward the alley and as soon as I was in view of his brother, I could see the white wings that contrasted with the dark ones that had just been keeping me warm. He seemed to lunge toward me in an instant. I felt the ground shake like an earthquake had caused everything around me to tremble. It knocked me down to the ground. When I reached out to lift myself back up, I saw the dark angel as he held his brother in his arms and carried him into the sky. They seemed to be fighting and I couldn't help but feel like the prey while one of them was the predator.

Running faster and faster, I couldn't seem to get away fast enough. The coffee shop appeared in the distance and I hesitated to go down the alley again. It would only lead me to a dead end I couldn't turn back from. I would be cornering myself. Although I barely knew the dark angel, Thanatos, I felt I could trust him for some reason.

I reluctantly headed down the alley and grasped the key in my hand, looking for a lock. The glow from the streetlights barely illuminated anything past the coffee shop. When I reached the end, I remembered the hole that was in the brick wall. It must have been a key hole.

The ground shook once more when I was just about to hold the key up to the opening. It dropped from my hands and made a ringing sound as soon as it hit the ground. When I turned, I could see the outline of two figures behind me. One of them towered over the other and looked as though he was trying to block the alley, but was being pushed deeper and deeper in. Despite the snow, my fingers felt like they were smothered in slippery butter. After feeling as though it took several minutes, I finally felt the key that had fallen and picked it up.

"Alice, go!" Thanatos yelled. In the corner of my eye, I could see just one figure now and he was just about to reach out to me when I finally turned the key in the hole and walked into the darkness, shutting out all that remained behind me.

HOSTAGE

10

Soft, feathery down encapsulated me into a world I never wanted to wake from. Wind gently blew in little by little, causing me to snuggle even more under the covers. I woke up in a bed that again looked like a tornado had come in and ripped through. The window was slightly opened and letting a draft in. I jumped out of bed with the covers still wrapped around me, nearly tripping over Toulouse as I rushed to close the window. The bitter cold sent chills down my spine and made me want to just stay in bed that much longer. I had to go into the station today and pretend like all was okay, but somehow I felt like I barely slept... I jumped where I stood, easily frightened, especially after the night's dreams. My phone went off. It had slid under the bed. When I kneeled down to reach for it, Toulouse swatted at my hand. I didn't blame him. I would be angry too if I had to live with me. He probably stayed far away from the bed when I was still dreaming.

"Hello," I answered quickly before I could bother looking at who was calling, afraid they would hang up if I took a second more.

"When are you coming to the station?" Jerome's calm voice asked. He got right to the point. I checked the time and realized I was already running later than usual. That would mean I'd have to stay even later, and I had promised dinner with both my parents after work.

"I'm leaving now," I said, leaving the comforter on the bed in a messy pile.

"Want a ride?" he asked.

"I'm already late. I don't want to make you late too," I replied.

"I'm outside."

At that, I hung up and realized I hadn't even changed into pajamas the night before. I still had the same clothes on. I threw my hair up in a messy bun and put glasses on to hide my eyes behind, hoping people wouldn't notice the dark circles as much. With the bitter cold, I decided to throw on a pair of jeans that smelled like they were still clean and a black shirt. I usually never took off my olive-colored trench coat, so that would keep me warm while I was outside, at least. I was surprised I didn't hear him, but as soon as I went outside, the loud thundering of his old car filled my ears.

"How did you know I was late?" I asked.

He shrugged his shoulders and stroked one hand through his dark hair, avoiding the answer. The rumbling from his exhaust matched my stomach's rumbles and reminded me of how hungry I was, clearly forgetting and being in too much of a rush to eat breakfast.

"You look like you didn't sleep at all," he noted as he peeled out of the driveway.

"Well thanks. You neither." I smirked and then frowned when we passed by several coffee shops. "I feel like I didn't sleep. I had such strange dreams…"

"Tell me about them," he said, alarmingly curious. I still felt like we were completely forgetting the fact he just showed up randomly and unannounced to pick me up for work, knowing I was running late somehow.

"It's just nonsense...it's all nonsense that doesn't make an ounce of sense," I said.

He gently touched my hand with his and an electric shock woke me up to where I no longer craved coffee at all. I scooted back in my seat and pretended like it didn't happen.

"Sorry," he said, acknowledging he just gave me a jolt. I wondered if he felt it as strongly as I had.

"What happened in your dream?" Jerome reminded me of what we had just been speaking about.

"It's just the same location every time. I am at a church...I think it's the one by that diner and I have never gone inside, but somehow I know exactly what it looks like. This dream was different though because it...well, there were no other people there. I was alone

except not really. There were two men, but they were

like Greek gods. And then one of them gave me a..."

Retelling what happened made me think of the key I

had used in the brick alley on a door I never knew

existed. I had on the same jacket I wore in the dream

and wondered if...I reached down into my pocket and

felt the metallic key. Its cold exterior gave me

goosebumps.

"And?" He made me shake out of my current state of

confusion. I dropped the key back in my pocket and

decided not to show it to him for some reason.

"And then all of a sudden I woke up," I said.

"Sometimes, you may not remember your full

dream. There has to be more to it," he said, reminding

me of how bad I was at lying. Although leaving out some parts...was that really lying?

"I just don't know what it all means...on top of the disappearances in town? I think it's all connected somehow."

"Maybe you need a break from it. Doing anything fun after work?"

"I promised Dad I would come over for dinner because I skipped out on it last night." I made a mental note not to forget.

"That should help you get your mind off things..." He trailed off as we entered the station's parking lot.

"What's wrong?" I could feel the tension in his usual calm and unshaken voice.

"The department is about to get a big call and I'm going to have to go soon. I'll see you later, okay?" he said as we both got out of his car. He slammed his door closed, and I followed, trying to keep up with him.

"Wait, how do you know?" I asked. As soon as we entered the station, the chief ran up to Jerome and I felt like an invisible ghost that just stood next to him while they spoke.

"Jerome, what took you so long?" the chief asked. "We have no time. There are many people whose lives are at risk in an apartment complex. It's an active shooter. It started from a domestic dispute." They both walked off, and the curiosity got the best of me. I wandered out into the parking lot and back to Jerome's car. I jiggled the handle and felt it was still unlocked. He must have forgotten in his rush to go inside.

I gently opened the passenger door and sat back inside, my seat still warm from before. As I watched the doors to the station, several police officers filed out and into their marked cars. Jerome came shortly after and got into his car, jumping at the sight of me. I could not feel more like a ghost than I already had.

"What are you doing here? I've got to go, didn't you hear?" he asked, starting the car.

"I'm coming," I stammered out, already buckling myself in to show I wasn't joking.

"If I had the time, I would help you out myself...but I can't be late," he said. "Just don't get into any trouble and stay outside when we go in."

WITNESS

11

Lights flashed from every direction and we had been following them this entire time. I had always been tucked away in the station and never felt the adrenaline rush all the officers I worked beside would experience daily. Jerome was an undercover cop, which was why he took his own car places, but had driven in the police cruisers before. I felt like his car could go from zero to sixty in the matter of seconds with how fast we raced to the scene. The cop cars created a pattern in the parking lot and a line, in a sense, as though they were trying to form a blockade against whoever was inside from escaping. A man came out from one room on the second floor and was holding a woman in his arms. It wasn't the slightest bit romantic since he had a gun pointed at her head, ready to shoot at any second. As soon as Jerome parked, he looked back at me and asked again for me not to leave the car.

"These things can go sideways sometimes...just don't come in, whatever you do..." he said, closing the door behind him. He walked past all the other police cars as if he had some sort of seniority over them suddenly and they just let him go. They had their doors opened to act as shields and were already positioned behind them, with their own guns out ready to shoot if need be. I could tell a few of them aimed right at the man's head, but knew they would not fire unless they had to because the woman's life was on the line.

Jerome was out of sight when he walked into the stairwell of the apartments, likely on the opposite side of the balcony. I slowly got out of the car and huddled behind one of the police cruisers and although there was a brief silence, the man took the girl back in the room with him, leaving the balcony bare once again.

"Is he okay in there?" I asked, confused why they allowed him to just go in like that and why it was suddenly quiet.

"Yeah, yeah...we do this all the time. He'll be fine," one of them said. I walked around the building and drifted into the stairwell that he must've taken to go up to the room. Everyone else had been standing down and staying in their same place. My curiosity got the best of me as I walked toward the room Jerome had warned me to stay away from. The cement floors were blank and washed out of any color while the maroon doors stood out, likely a fashion from the 70s.

The door burst open just as I was about to put my ear against it to listen in, and I quickly backed away. The lady who was just being held at gunpoint locked eyes with me. Her hazel eyes seemed to be drowning in a mess of wet mascara that streamed down her cheeks. When she whisked past me, I could even feel both her relief and urgency in the escape she just made. But where was Jerome? In the next moment, a loud gunshot echoed from out of the room. I felt my heart as it sank in my chest, for I didn't know who the gun was aimed at. Either way, it would have been a tragedy. Without thinking, I rushed into the room and in the mess of everything, looking strikingly similar to the tornado that seemed to frequent my own room, I saw the man who had his gun at the start while Jerome stood over him. He seemed to not hear me come in, but remained there with his hand clasped around the man's as he lay there, lifeless, on the floor. I wanted to run up to Jerome and comfort him for what he had just had to witness, but couldn't help but feel something stopping me. I had only ever felt like this one other time... when I was paralyzed in my dream. I was forced to watch everything play out, and that was one of the worst feelings of them all. To see everything in front of you happening...you want to help, you want to do something...but you are just paralyzed. In many ways, this was an even worse torture than actually being the victim that lay before my eyes.

All was silent while Jerome mumbled something that was much too quiet for me to hear. His hand clasped around the man on the floor, and I wasn't sure why. After what felt like a while, he gently placed the man's hand beside his limp body and got up to turn toward me. It was then that I no longer felt paralyzed, and a newfound energy overtook me from just his simple gaze. What shocked me the most was that he was perfectly calm. When we stared at one another, the door burst in from behind me and officers flooded into the room. I was pushed out of the way. I went the opposite direction and back down the stairs to see if I could at least question the woman who had been the initial hostage. The crime scene unit would likely be in the apartment room for hours investigating.

Outside, just a few detectives were on their phones and talking. There was no sign of the woman. I walked over to the ambulance, which had been parked just behind the blockade of police cars, to see if she was sitting inside.

"Can we help you?" one of the EMTs said, who was standing with his arms crossed beside the back doors to the ambulance.

"Uh..yes. I was looking for the hostage; I needed to ask her a few questions." I grabbed my notebook out of my bag to look more official.

"You don't think it's a little too soon? You could give her a chance to breathe, ya know…" he said.

"Everything is fresh in her mind right now; otherwise, trust me, I would give her all the time she needed."

He opened up the doors, and I saw the same shaken girl I had seen moments before the gunshot went off. She held a cup of what appeared to be coffee in her hands. A thick plaid blanket was draped over her for comfort.

"Ma'am...do you have a minute?" I peered in.

She nodded. Her loose blonde curls hung down to her chest and nearly dipped in the mug she held. She looked like she had just walked through a storm and somehow come out alive. I pushed myself up into the back and sat across from her, afraid being too close would only make her more hesitant about speaking with me.

"What's your name?" I asked, trying to start with the most basic questions I possibly could.

"Clara," she answered after a long pause.

"That's a pretty name. What do you do for work?" I wrote her name in quick cursive on the notepad so I could remember.

"I'm a nurse."

"That's got to be very difficult," I said the obvious.

"Yeah, especially when you meet someone who...who..." she choked up on their name. I moved my seat right next to her and began rubbing her back. This was something my mom always did for me when I was feeling upset. I knew it couldn't solve anything for her, but felt like it was better than doing nothing.

"Take deep breaths...it's okay," I said. She was shaking so much that splotches of coffee fell out of the mug and onto the floor. I took it from her and set it beside me on the seat.

"It's just too much at once...and I don't understand it," she said.

"It's not something we can ever understand, I'm afraid."

"The man…Oliver…he was fine. He was always fine. But it was like something overtook him and he was no longer himself. He was no longer Oliver," she sobbed and held her head in her hands. I realized Oliver must've been the shooter.

"So he never threatened you before?" I asked, handing her a box of tissues that was nearby in the ambulance.

"Never. He was the sweetest man," she said, grabbing a bunch of tissues from the box. Wet mascara quickly turned the white of the tissues black and smudged on her cheeks. "But that's not what is confusing me the most…"

"What is?"

"I don't know how to explain it. This thing I had never seen before…when he walked back into the room with me in his arms, there was something that I'm going to sound like an idiot describing," she said.

"Was there another person there?" I asked.

"I don't think you could call them a person. Can I use your notebook for a second?" she asked, hands shaky as she took the pen and notebook from my lap that I had stopped writing notes in, too curious to break my focus.

She lightly sketched an outline of a figure that appeared to be a man. His bare torso was toned in her shading and he stood up tall. I would've mistaken this for just another guy if not for what she began sketching at the end. Dark wings protruded out of each of his shoulders. As she shaded them in more, I felt my heart sink in my chest. Was this a dream?

Just when I was about to ask her more, Jerome showed up outside the ambulance. The girl flinched and began crying uncontrollably again. EMTs rushed in and I left her with my card, walking out with the notebook and pen with even more questions than I had before.

SILENCE

12

The silence wrapped around me as I struggled to keep my thoughts at bay. Part of me felt like I should say everything, but the other questioned him and who he truly was. As soon as Clara caught sight of Jerome, she completely lost it. I wondered what happened up in the apartment before she went running out of there. I stared out the window when we headed back to the station, afraid to look back at him...afraid of what he might say or do. I wasn't even sure why I had gotten in the car with him in the first place. I was too trusting of others... if he truly wanted, he could've done anything.

MARISSA D'ANGELO

But in that room, he was so calm. Despite the death that lay out before him, it was almost inhumane to have kept his composure so well at the time. None of it made sense.

"So...you're awfully quiet," he broke the silence.

"Mhm," I said, not wanting to engage in conversation; hesitant of what I might say.

"Why didn't you tell me you do the complete opposite of what you are told?" he asked.

"Oh, I'm sorry... I didn't know that you controlled me." I felt my eyebrows furrow in, angry at the fact he was questioning me when it took everything in me not to do the same back.

"Sometimes, there are more victims. I just didn't want you to be one of them," he said.

"Why were you holding his hand?" I finally asked.

136

"You saw that?"

"You didn't answer my question…" I turned my focus to him. His hands gripped the steering wheel tightly; veins nearly protruded out of his arms.

"What did you see?" he answered with another question.

"The gunshot went off and when I walked in, he was on the floor…you stood beside him as you held his hand. I can't understand why you would do something like that," I said.

"I felt some remorse for the life lost…" he trailed off.

"But you didn't even know him."

"It doesn't matter. A life lost is a life lost." He pressed his lips together as if he wanted to say more, but held back.

My sunken heart suddenly felt more relieved, but also sorry I had questioned him so much. It must have been hard for him to be the first one in the situation and see death laid out before him. I still had so many questions and wondered what else Clara could tell me about what happened.

We pulled into the station and I unbuckled my seatbelt, ready to head in and brush off what had just happened. The only thing was, I couldn't forget. Some things are worth forgetting and not paying any mind to any longer... I wished I could make Jerome forget, too. The pain of seeing someone die—let alone kill themselves—in front of you was gut-wrenching. All Jerome had ever tried to do was help me, a stranger, whom he had barely known. And I suspected him of the worst.

I pulled out my lunch from my bag before getting out of the car and passed him the chips.

"Here. I know it won't make it better, but these are really yummy and I thought you could use them for your lunch," I said as I gave him a smile.

"You don't have to do that. This is your lunch," he insisted and pushed them back my way.

"No, no. Take them. Can't have just one." I winked.

When I left the car, I felt so corny with the remark I had just made that my face suddenly felt red in embarrassment. I was glad he couldn't see me as I headed into the station, not daring to look back.

Inside, the phones rang uncontrollably, and I muttered under my breath while I fumbled for my badge to get behind the counter. Scanning it didn't seem to do the trick; I pressed it more firmly up to the sensor and the satisfying beep of clearance unlocked the door for a short time. I stepped forward and entered the staff area. Just as I had left it, my desk was open on the lefthand side. The one beside it was still empty and cleared of its contents. Izzy and I would come in together and get all of our work done. When she was around, I would've never had as big a pile of papers as I currently did. Seeing her desk each day and knowing she may never be at it again made my stomach turn. My desk matched all the others except for the piles of papers on it of work I had stayed late to finish, but never got to. I sighed and wondered what life would have been like if I had chosen another job.

"Late start today?" Lance asked.

He was one of those annoying coworkers that always tried nosing into your business no matter the time of day. I felt like I always had to look over my shoulder for him. If I made a mistake, he would be the first one to catch it. I didn't want to explain how I went with an undercover cop to an active hostage situation. He would've asked so many questions and been relentless for so long. It was better off not to give him more to talk about than he already had.

"Good morning to you too," I reluctantly responded.

"I didn't know we could just come into work whenever we wanted."

"That's too bad. You must be on a different schedule than me," I smirked.

I heard him grunt and roll back towards his own desk with his chair, crazily typing away God knows what on his keyboard. He was probably pretending to work. His thick-rimmed glasses looked like they were borrowed from Clark Kent, but looked the complete opposite. Lance had dirty blond hair he often forgot to cut; long, wavy strands reached his shoulders. When I looked at him, I couldn't help but stare at his furry eyebrows; they could be caterpillars that went to sleep on his face.

"Izzy, if only you were here..." I muttered under my breath.

"What was that?" His chair let out a squeak. I felt great empathy for that chair, having to be stuck with him each and every day.

"Wasn't talking to you."

The phone at my desk saved me from any further conversation.

"Yes?" I answered it right away.

"That guy giving you a hard time?" I could hear Jerome's voice on the other end and looked back to find him sitting at his desk, which was much farther away in the station. He was smiling and rolling back and forth in his chair as if he knew just how sly he was. It was perfect timing.

"Am I going to be able to get any work done around here?" I asked, lifting the top file off of the pile that just kept increasing on my desk. It was the hostage file from earlier. I hadn't remembered grabbing this one...

"Just thought you needed an excuse not to talk to him," he chuckled.

"Thank you," I said, flipping through the several pages that filled the Manila envelope. It turned out the suspect had prior arrests and domestic disputes.

"I'll be here if you need me."

"Jerome, I appreciate it. It must have been hard on you this morning. Enjoy those chips," I reminded him and hung the phone up.

The man's name was Oliver. The pages in the very back displayed his records from when he was just a child. Both of his parents seemed to have given up on him at birth and he was in and out of several orphanages his entire life. Throughout high school, he struggled with getting suspended time after time.

I grabbed my bag and headed out of the station to go back to the scene of the crime, curious why it went down the way it had. Clara said something overcame Oliver, and she had never seen him like this before. Even though he had a troubled past, he turned his life around and even met a girl. So then why did he hold her at gunpoint that day only to kill himself?

FLASHBACK

13

Unfortunately, having been given a ride from Jerome, I had to call a taxi so I could be as discreet as possible. No one had followed me out of the building, which was good, but there was still a chance every movement of mine was being carefully watched. The wind gently whistled in the silence of the parking lot while I sat on a bench beside a tree. Memories flooded through my mind of this same bench when Izzy was still around. I needed to figure out a way to get her back. Part of me felt she was still out there and that hope was the only thing that kept me going. I stared out at the tree for a moment and let my mind wander.

"Alice! Alice!" Izzy yelled up to me while I sat on the bench. "You'll never guess what happened!"

I turned toward her, and she was running from the parking lot. Whenever I was a little early to work or just needed a break from being in the station all day, I would come out here to think and write in my journal. Izzy knew where to find me.

"What is it?" I asked, intrigued.

"He finally asked me out!" She was smiling so widely. The last time I saw her that happy was in high school when she was asked out to prom by her boyfriend back then.

"It's about time!" I was almost sure she had been friend-zoned, but she kept trying with this guy that she

met at the coffee shop. She wouldn't dare tell me his name, but would go on and on about him until late at night.

She twirled around and around in circles as if she were a ballerina. My nonexistent love life envied how she felt right now, but I was happy for her, too.

"Now we've gotta get you with someone," she had said.

"I'm perfectly fine the way I am. Besides, I have Toulouse. He's a great companion." I continued doodling in my journal. She walked over and closed the journal on me, abruptly. "Uhm, excuse you!" I snatched it and held it close to my chest.

"Oooh, what have you got in there?" she asked, reaching for the journal again while I darted away. I got just a few feet away before she stopped where she stood and I continued holding my precious pages close to me.

"It's nothing."

"Come on, you're blushing!"

"Weren't we talking about how excited you are with what's his name?" I tried to change the topic, wondering why the spotlight had so easily shifted to me.

"It's Jerome, isn't it? From the station? Come on, just ask him out already. Or introduce yourself at least!!" She knew me well, and that was why she was my best friend.

"Oh, please...he doesn't even know I exist. If he was interested, he would've introduced himself."

"What will it hurt if you just say hello?" She folded her arms over her chest, clearly irritated with how stubborn I was being.

"And just stand there awkwardly? No...no..." I had imagined it in my mind. I would walk over to him and barely be able to get the words out. Perhaps I'd even choke

on my own spit and humiliate myself in front of everyone at the station.

"You always stare at him at the gym inside the station! Don't deny it!" She inched closer to me and smiled.

"Colleagues can't date."

"He's in a different department!"

"Still."

"You're so stubborn. Just think on it," she insisted, and we got into my car together since we had carpooled. It was always fun going back to our place together to just watch movies and relax. I never wanted it to end.

I snapped out of it when I heard a car pull in nearby. A yellow and black checkered car pulled up, and I waved their way so they knew I was out there. The thought lingered in my mind for a moment more of what would have happened if I had taken Izzy's advice.

When I glanced back at the station's entrance, I was relieved to see no one was there. The driver faced forward and didn't lean back when he spoke, so I couldn't tell what he looked like, but he had darker hair.

"Where to, miss?" he asked, wasting no time.

I gave him the address to my place so I could get my car and just go where I needed to go.

"You work at the station?" He seemed like he was trying to make conversation. I could barely focus since my mind was all over the place.

"Yes," I answered. "I've been there a few years now."

"It must be stressful."

"Sometimes, but only when you're given a case that sends you on a wild goose chase." I was referring to the never ending scavenger hunt I had been on with the disappearances. It had been a few days since the last one. It was only a matter of time until the next one.

"What do you mean?" The signal came on in the car and he turned onto the main road.

"Some assignments that you are given end up being cold cases after a while of searching for answers. That is one of the biggest downfalls at the station, along with lives lost." I felt my heart sink when I thought of Oliver from that morning. Although it seemed like forever ago, the pain was still fresh.

"Oh yeah. I watch *Criminal Minds*. Good show."

"It is a good show, but things do not happen anywhere near as fast as they do in each episode. In real life, some crimes go unsolved for years and the abundance of paperwork is just one of the many hassles to go through."

"So, why did you start working there?" His interest in my work life was questionable, but I figured he was just trying to make the time fly by faster. It was working.

"I wanted to help any way I could. Why did you become a taxi driver?"

"I guess the same reason."

"Well, our jobs are quite different. I should've just become a taxi driver. It seems less of a hassle and no murders to worry about."

"That is for sure. Is this your place?" We pulled up to my townhome.

"Yep, that's me."

"It was nice talking with you. Keep your head up, things will work out." I felt like he was my grandfather giving me advice as a young child.

"Thanks, I appreciate it. You too."

I gave him a folded up twenty and left, walking right to my car instead of going inside the house. As much as I wanted to just stay home and snuggle under my blankets for the rest of eternity, I had to get to the crime scene to look at it one last time. Something in me told me I missed something.

RETRACING

14

Curiosity has always been one of my greatest downfalls in life and it didn't help that I had several cases without leads. There had to be a connection with this hostage case despite it not being a disappearance. Lately, all the strange happenings seemed connected in town. There must've been something I had missed.

Yellow caution tape riddled the balcony where the man—Oliver—had stood. I brought my badge with me in case anyone asked me questions, but noticed there were only a few people there from the station. It looked like most of the detectives had obtained what they needed for the case and filed out. It was strange because a lot of these people I hadn't seen before at the station. As I continued on to go up the stairwell, a rush of emotions overcame me. The adrenaline rush that I had felt just a few hours prior, unknowing what was going to happen and the push that I had to go up there even though I wasn't allowed.

"Ma'am, do you need something? This is a crime scene," a tall woman said. She wore a bulletproof vest and black khakis. She looked like one of those people you would see on an investigation show…except they were usually from a higher branch than the police department. Maybe FBI…

"I was on the scene when the hostage situation was still active. I've come to gather a few more notes." I showed her my badge.

156

"Well, there's not much to really find. But have at it..." she said. I wasn't sure what she meant, but walked on anyway, going up the stairs much more easily than I had before. There wasn't much of a rush anymore. Something seemed off and different, though. I just couldn't place it.

Two agents who wore the same gear as the lady at the bottom of the stairwell stood outside the room, talking. I showed them my badge without saying anything and one of them nodded, but the other moved in front of the door and questioned me.

"What more is there to find?" one of them asked.

"I was here earlier when the man was just laying on the carpet in there. It was a suicide, but the hostage made it out okay. I just wanted to check the scene one more time for anything I may have missed," I said again.

At this point, I could've recited all my reasonings in my sleep. I wondered who else would question me.

"What man?" The other agent, who had originally nodded for me to go through, asked.

"Oliver."

"And where is he now?"

"You tell me. At the morgue?" I questioned back, frustrated and confused.

"You don't know?" one of them asked.

I put my hands on my hips and waited for them to tell me. In a way, I felt these were the Tweedle Dee and Tweedle Dumb gate keepers from Alice in Wonderland. They just kept beating around the bush.

"When the detectives and officers came in, the man was gone. One of them...oh, what's his name again, Jeff?"

THE VANISHED

"It started with a J...same letter as my name." I looked at his vest and saw Joshua sewn in. "Unusual name. Oh yeah, Jerome. Jerome said he was there one minute and then vanished," Joshua thought aloud.

"What!"

"You'd think you would know. You were here, weren't you?!" Joshua asked.

"When I was last here, the man had shot himself with his gun while Clara managed to get away just a few moments before," I admitted to them.

"Well, that's not what everyone else found. Go on in. We're closing the doors in just a few minutes. We'll be out here if you need anything," Joshua said while the other one nodded.

I ducked under the yellow caution tape that marked off the doorway despite the door being wide open. In

159

the center of the room was a red blood stain from Oliver

bleeding out on the floor. But he had been holding

Jerome's hand, so how could he have just vanished into

thin air like that? I pulled out my notebook, opening up

to the page Clara had drawn the black-winged figure

on. Flipping to the next available page, I wrote some

questions that now swarmed my mind.

Where did Oliver go?

What items were uncovered at the scene?

What was the possible motive?

Why didn't Jerome tell me?!

The sharp point of my pencil nearly ripped the page

when I wrote the last question in all caps. I had to talk

to Jerome. He was so quiet when we went back to the

station; I could tell there was something he wasn't

telling me. A blood stain with no body? But I had seen Oliver lying there, lifeless.

Behind the couch in the room, there was a black speck that caught my attention. I couldn't place what it was. I walked towards it cautiously and looked behind me to make sure no one was coming in. Rounding the dried pool of blood that stained the middle of the floor, I winced at the sight of it, but held my breath as I continued on. The musty, horrid smell of death lingered in the room from before. It was instantly pushed to the back of my mind when I found the missing piece to the puzzle I had been searching for all along to connect this with the other disappearances.

The black feather. This one wasn't as long as the one I had found in the alley where Jack vanished. But it was still longer than any bird I had ever seen before. Could my dreams be right? It was the only thing that made sense. There was something else that lurked among all of us and we couldn't even tell. But why did it keep taking everyone? Jerome had to have seen something...

"We've got to close up. Finish up in there," one agent called in from the other side of the tape. I wanted to take the newfound evidence with me, but had no idea where I would put it. My backpack wasn't nearly long enough to hold it. I took off my coat and wrapped it up within so it looked like I was just holding onto my coat and nothing else. Or I hoped it would, at least.

"Ok, ok. I'm all set."

"You getting warm in the freezing temperatures we've been having?" an agent asked.

"Oh yeah, just a bit. Maybe I'm coming down with something."

"Well, don't give whatever you have to us," they said as they inched away. I had to stifle my laugh; I was never very good at lying and whenever I did, I would always get caught out in it.

"Well, I'll be on my way then..." I said and didn't look back, afraid it would lead to more suspicions. At the bottom of the steps, the female agent, who acted as a guard of the stairwell, was still there.

"Find anything?" She heard me coming before I even walked past her.

"Not really. You were right, there wasn't much to find..." I was scarily getting better at this.

"If you need anything, here's my card. See anything else suspicious, let me know. Okay?" She handed me her card that she already had ready.

"Thanks." I fumbled for it, nearly dropping my coat and revealing the piece of evidence I stashed away. I was sure it would've been a felony to conceal evidence from an agent. I dropped it into my bag and readjusted the coat I held between my arm and waist. When I finally made it back to my car, I breathed a sigh of relief. I had to open up my coat on the passenger seat to see that it was really true that I found another black feather and not just a figment of my imagination. I could feel my heart racing in my chest when the truth was unveiled and more questions flooded my mind.

QUESTIONING

15

"Have you seen Jerome?" I asked Lance as soon as I got into the station, seeing Jerome's empty desk.

"I don't know. Maybe he's at the station gym like he usually is," he answered, clearly annoyed I interrupted whatever he was doing.

"Ok thanks." I plopped my bag down beside my desk and grabbed my gym clothes I kept in the drawer for the times I planned to workout, but never did. I wasn't exactly sure how to confront Jerome about this, especially when I hadn't exactly ruled him out as a suspect. I walked all the way through the main lobby of the station and toward the back, where the department had just installed a bunch of gym equipment in a spare room. We had received a grant to fund everything in here and I thought it was really helpful, especially with how stressed out the job could make us. There were just a few times I made use of it, but kept telling myself I would make it a routine. Life seemed to get in the way, though.

A row of treadmills lined the front of the room beside a long mirror that took over the entire wall. Behind them was a matching row of cycling machines. In the back were various yoga mats. Jerome wasn't using any of the machines in the room. I walked past a few people as they barely noticed my presence, music blaring so loud that I could hear it from their headphones. Adjacent to the machine room, was the locker room, where we could keep our things, and then shower. I continued through the women's locker room and walked to the closest locker so I could quickly store my clothes there. If there were ever a day to work out, it would be today. There wasn't much I could do without getting the story straight from Jerome. It frustrated me because whenever I wanted to find him, I couldn't. But when I didn't need him, he would just appear all of a sudden. A good workout on the treadmill would relieve some of the tension that had built up surrounding all the disappearances. With slim black yoga pants and a tank top that had our station number on it, I slipped my boots in the locker and tied up the sneakers I hadn't worn in so long. I grabbed both sides of my hair and put it up high in a ponytail so it was out of my face. I always felt I looked ten years younger whenever I did this...like I belonged in middle or high school. The others wouldn't notice, though; I doubt they even knew who I was. I kept quiet at the station. Went in, did my work, then left when it was all done. With that mindset, there were fewer problems between coworkers...well, except for Lance. He was always a pain in the ass, no matter how much I ignored him.

I plugged in my headphones and started walking at a slow speed, staring at the various buttons I could press. I wished it was warmer out so I could just go walking on one of the many trails we had nearby. It would be less boring. When I looked up at the mirror, I saw Jerome's reflection. He was in the weight room just behind all the cycling machines. I could only see one of his arms and just barely his head. But those biceps were something I just couldn't miss, even in a reflection. I don't remember ever seeing him with only a tank top on before. But I could tell it was him. He moved to the side and made eye contact with me in the mirror from far away. I broke my gaze, embarrassed. When I looked back, he was still watching me and smiling. I could feel my cheeks grow red. He gestured for me to come back to the weight room with him.

After walking a few more steps, I finally found the guts to go back there. *Alice, focus. He's just a colleague, nothing more, and you need to find a time to question him.*

"I didn't know you worked out here," he said.

"Me neither," I admitted, trying to look at his face, but finding it impossible not to look at the rest of him.

"Do you want to try some weights back here?"

"Uhm, sure, why not?" I couldn't help but think of the questions I wanted to ask him, but was so distracted by everything else. He gave me a pair of smaller weights and I felt my arms sink down as soon as I took them from him. He laughed.

"It's really helpful even if you walk in place on the treadmill while holding them. You can do some stretches too with them. It makes the workout that much better on your body." I could see him looking me up and down. I decided to do some lunges on the mat while he continued lifting the weights that he had. The sweat on his body trailed down his neck and chest. I found it hard to continue doing the lunges, but was glad I had something to hold on to for the time being.

"So, you didn't tell me..." I started, trying to figure out how to phrase my question.

"Tell you what?" he asked.

"You didn't tell me that Oliver disappeared. I saw you there with him holding his hand after he..." My words trailed off when I felt him come up beside me and took the weights out of my hands. He set them aside and took my hands in his.

"Alice..."

"That's a key piece of information in the case. And you left it out completely. Why?"

"You're on the case?"

"No...but I was there. I'd like to know what else happened and if it's connected."

"I don't think so."

"But then, where did he go? He was just gone in the blink of an eye? You must've seen something leading up to it."

"Alice...there are some things we don't understand, and the disappearance is one of those things."

The way he said my name was as soft as velvet. It just rolled off his tongue so delicately. He gently squeezed my hands.

"Look at me." His tone was now serious and stern. When I looked into his gentle eyes, I couldn't help but to get closer to him.

"What?" I asked.

"If you are ever at an active shooter and hostage situation, please listen to the advice I give you. I can't lose you."

"But what am I to you?"

"You're too important. I can't lose you."

His arms extended around me as he pulled me in close. He rested his head at the nape of my neck and my body pressed into him. His breath wafted across my neck, and it felt like his lips were about to press into me. Just when they slightly touched my skin, he pulled back and looked down at the ground. I took his chin in my hand, forcing him to look at me again as he had before.

"Tell me what happened. Tell me everything." I knew he was holding back, and I wanted to break down the wall he had up.

"I can't."

"Why not?"

"It'll only hurt you. You can't get involved in this."

"I won't tell anyone," I promised.

"This isn't the time...or place." He looked over at the people who were still on their treadmill machines.

"Well, then let's meet later."

"Dinner?" he asked. Would that be a date? I thought on it but then remembered the rain check I had given my parents for missing dinner the previous night and just taking off.

"Oh, I told my dad I would be over for dinner. I can't tonight. Maybe after?" I asked, wishing I could just cancel on my parents, but knew it would let them down.

"Yeah, sure. Just text me when you're done," he said. Just then, more colleagues walked in to use the fitness room. I moved away from Jerome and lifted the weights he had given me.

"Thanks for showing me how to use these." I gave them back to him.

"No problem. Anytime," he said, playing along with me. I smiled and walked away, glad he was going to resolve some questions I had. I felt like I was finally on

the same page with someone after all this time.

BACK TO THE ROOTS

16

The day's events tired me out. I nearly drove home on autopilot, but knowing I was going to meet with Jerome later gave me the energy I needed to pull through. It was already sunset. Orange hues streamed out into the world as the sun completed its descent in the sky. When I got to my parents' house, dinner was already set on the table as soon as I walked in. I wanted to tell them everything, but the problem was, I still didn't even know *what* was going on. But I was closer to solving the case.

"How was your day?" Mom asked while getting glasses for the table. I walked over and helped her.

"I don't even know where to begin," I said. The active shooter? Boy, Dad would love to hear about that... He'd make me quit working at the station and quite possibly wrap me in bubble wrap to keep anything bad from happening to me. Or should I have started at the black-winged creature that Clara drew in my notebook?

"I had a bit of a long day, too, at work." She set the glasses down and walked over to the fridge to get some drinks. "We had several people code, and we tried to resuscitate them, but were unable to revive any of them."

"It sounds like we might be tied on bad days. Where's dad?" I asked.

"Oh, he went upstairs to wash up. He said he'll be right down. So what happened with you today?"

"I'll explain at dinner. I'm going to go get Dad," I called back, already walking up the steps toward the master bedroom of our house. I could hear the video he was watching on his phone already.

"Bear versus lion. See who will win," the narrator's deep tone announced. I couldn't help but giggle to myself at his choice in videos. At this rate, he would never be down if I hadn't gone up to get him.

"Dad, dinner is ready!" I knocked on the door.

"Alice, you're here!!" he cried. The video was still playing, but he burst out of the bedroom with it in his hand and gave me a big hug.

"Oh, too tight!" I shouted.

"How was your day today?" he asked, attempting to pause the video with his fat fingers, but he continuously replayed it, pressing the button too many times. I took it from him and stopped it. He gave me an innocent smile and took the phone back from me.

"It was really hard, but there were some good times," I said, unable to stop myself from blushing.

"Oh, no...who's the guy that I need to have a talk with?" he asked, already protective.

"It's no one," I insisted.

"I guess I'll just have to find out my own way," he said, descending the steps.

"What're you going to do??"

"Hey, what's for dinner?" Dad asked Mom, changing the subject.

"Tell him not to butt into my business!" I changed it right back.

"What're you two talking about?" she said, clearly confused. "We're having breaded chicken for dinner with some mashed potatoes and broccoli. Your favorite."

"Well, not the broccoli part, but the others I'll take," Dad said.

"Okay, I met a guy and Dad found out and now he wants to know who he is so he can interrogate him. We haven't even gone on a date!!" I summed up everything for her.

"You should invite him over!" Mom said. I rolled my eyes. They would definitely scare him away if I did that, and we weren't even a thing. I thought about the dark angel and how he made me feel. But then Jerome. It was almost like one had something the other did not.

"No, thank you!! Maybe someday." I settled on a maybe. "Anyway, there's a lot happening at the station right now. It seems I was right about the disappearances being connected." Dad took two giant spoonfuls of potatoes and plopped them onto his plate, then handed the spoon over to me so I could do the same.

"How do you know?" Mom asked while Dad was busy stuffing his face.

"At both scenes, there was a similar black feather and they just seem to disappear into thin air, bringing nothing with them. And it's not just any black feather. It's the longest I have ever seen. It doesn't look like it belongs to a bird. Something else."

"Did you tell anyone at the station about the connections?" Mom asked.

"I can't work the case because of my connection with Izzy. It's too personal of a connection. They won't allow me."

"That's my girl. So you're just doing it anyway." Dad took a break from the potatoes. I grinned. We were both one and the same, in that when someone told us not to do something we were passionate about, we would do it anyway. Stubborn, but passionate.

"I feel like she's just going to be forgotten if someone doesn't try to solve it. Similar things just keep happening, too."

"I get that," Mom chimed in. "I think I would do the same if I were in your shoes. Just be careful. You don't know who you are dealing with."

"I know, Mom."

"Here, take this." Dad handed me a small bag.

"What is it?"

"Just open it."

I pulled out a small black bottle of something and read the inscription. Pepper spray.

"Do you really think I'm going to be needing this?" I asked.

"You never know. And even if you didn't work at the station, it is still a good thing to have on you, just in case."

I stood up and walked over to Dad, gave him a hug. Then to Mom.

"Thank you guys. I really appreciate it. The dinner was amazing." I piled up the dishes and started doing them so Mom wouldn't have to.

"If you wanna stay, we could watch a movie?" Dad suggested. I promised Jerome I would meet him, though. But I couldn't tell them that. They would think I was up to no good.

"I've got to get up early for work. Let's pick a movie to watch this weekend."

"Okay, text us when you get home so we know you got there safely," Mom said.

"I will," I said and went out the back door.

THE TRUTH

17

I couldn't help but feel a deep warmth inside my chest when I left, but it was bittersweet. Part of me wished to remain a child in their home and just stay there forever. But the other part knew I had to get an apartment so I could create a life of my own. The challenges that came from obtaining a sense of independence surmounted everything. Gradually, I got used to it. When I first made the decision to leave, neither of my parents were happy. I think Dad was in denial that I was getting older and I would always just be his little girl in his eyes. But Mom kind of sensed it was about time I moved out. Living so close made it easier.

The moon was bright in the sky and illuminated the grounds below me in an ethereal glow. There was no time to waste since I had to get back to see Jerome. I looked up and saw various bats glide out from a nearby tree, squeaking like mice. I instantly held my hands up to my hair, protecting myself if they decided to swoop down on me. Luckily, they continued on into the distance as night swept them away into its dark abyss. When I looked out at the forest behind my parents' house, I remembered all the times I played capture the flag in the backyard. My friends and I would team up against one another and then try to steal each other's flag. At some point, the game would end in me giggling uncontrollably on the ground. But it had been daytime back then. At night, the forest seemed to be a completely different place, forbidden and mysterious. I shuffled for my keys as I walked around the fence that led to the front. I knew they were somewhere in my bag because I could hear the clank of the metal against everything else. When I looked up again, I saw the dark wings in the sky. This time they were not from any bat, but a much bigger being. A being that the long black feathers I found at each scene had belonged to. I couldn't see his face since it was too dark, but knew the wings from my dreams. I ran the other way toward the back door, banging on it repeatedly to be let back in. No one was answering.

"Mom, Dad! Please, let me in!" I threw my body against the door. When I walked over to the nearby window, I peered in and could see both of my parents sitting at the table, frozen in place and unblinking. I banged on the window, peering behind me to find the creature was nowhere in sight. Both of my parents were in a trance, like the people had been in my dream several nights ago. I couldn't go around front again because that was where he was. Instead, I ran toward the forest that had always been forbidden to me during the night. As soon as I felt the biggest tree, I clung to it and hoped it could shield me from whatever danger there was now coming my way.

Shaking uncontrollably, I somehow pulled out my phone so I could call Jerome. He was my only hope, although I wasn't sure what he could possibly do against the being that now lurked in the night.

"Please pick up, please pick up," I said while finding his contact information to call him. A rustle in the distance made me jump as I ran even further into the forest. Without a single ring, the call went right to voicemail.

"Hey, you've reached Jerome. Please leave me a mess—" I hung up and tried again. I kept trying. Was he in a trance like my parents had been? The rustling in the distance seemed to get even closer. Moonlight trickled down and reflected against a pond I was so thankful I hadn't fallen right into. Dark wings concealed the light that there once was, encapsulating any remaining glimmer of hope I had within, and I shifted to the other side of the tree. I had to hold my hand over my mouth, afraid he would hear my heavy breaths. The only way to escape him was to get into my car and drive back home. I peeked out from the tree and heard his footsteps draw away. He must've thought I was headed in another direction. This was my chance.

I started running as fast as I could back toward the front of their house, uncaring whether or not he could hear me at this point. My arms were fully extended so I could feel for trees or anything else that stood in my way, masked by the darkness. A powerful gust of wind blew through the night's frigid air and forced me to push my hands into my pockets, feeling like they had already turned blue. The numbness spread throughout my body and I, too, felt like paralysis crept all over my body until one wrong step and I went flying forward, nearly landing face first in the mud. For a moment, I was uncontrollably falling, bracing for the impact that would surely make me scream out in pain. But I didn't land on the hard, uneven ground that was riddled with rocks. Instead, a warm embrace broke my fall, as if he had been waiting for me to slip up somewhere. My face pressed into his rock-hard chest and I looked up, paranoid for the truth that laid right there. In the corner of my eye, I could see his dark wings that haunted my dreams and each crime scene I had gone to. *Was this it? Would I be the next one to disappear?*

"Alice." It was like smooth velvet that gently rolled off his tongue like he had said it many times before. I looked into his ocean blue eyes and knew I finally found the last piece of the puzzle I had been looking for.

Jerome.

DEJA VU

18

Those dark wings wrapped around me as I suddenly felt warm again, just like I had in my dream. Not even a speck of moonlight glistened in as his wings blocked out everything, even the sound of the wind whispering through the forest. Owl calls echoed amongst the trees, then dispersed into nothingness. A deep, desolate darkness that I had felt on the inside for the longest time just remained on the outside. As soon as I saw his eyes, things made sense, but then more questions arose all at once.

"We don't have much time," he said, extending his wings out again as if he was about to take flight.

"I'm not going anywhere until you tell me what is going on." I planted my feet in the ground and tried to stay put even though I knew he was likely stronger than me and could lift me as if I were as light as a feather. He slowly inched over and I backed away, hesitant.

In the next second, I felt his arm wrap around me while his other was on my waist. I could no longer feel the ground beneath my feet. When I looked down, we were at least a few feet up. I clung onto him, feeling as though I was a defenseless lamb while he was the lion, having the ability to maul me at any moment. My life; the entirety of my being lay in his hands.

"I'll explain everything, but first we must go," he explained, soaring higher in the sky as I nearly dug my nails into his skin, latching on with everything I could. "I'm not going to let you fall."

"What about my parents?" I asked, wondering if they were still in the trance.

"They're fine. It's you they want," he simply said, with little more explanation.

"Me?"

"Shh, we need to go somewhere else. Then we'll talk." He turned me around mid-air and I nearly screamed, if not for his constant shushing. I felt his arms wrap around my chest and stomach as if they were a seatbelt in a car; my legs and arms dangled down as I watched the small flickers of light from the buildings below. The city I had known my entire life seemed so quiet and small from above. Bustling cars in the busy streets looked like tiny ants shuffling around this way and that. I could barely even hear any car horns blaring or ambulances and police cars rushing down the streets, as I normally would. Being up so high irked me and I wished to be on the ground again. I felt my stomach turn in fear that I would fall at any moment. At the thought of falling to my death, I felt his grip on me grow even tighter. He slowed down and in a matter of seconds, I felt my feet touch the ground again. I stumbled, trying to remember how to walk. Before me was an old library that had been abandoned for years. In high school, I remember all the kids tempting one another to go inside. Rumors of ghosts passed on and in order to be considered for certain cliques, you'd have to pass their test of breaking in. I remember Izzy had tried fitting into one clique and just when they asked her to go in the creepy library, she didn't even care anymore about being in the popular crowd.

"We're going in?" I whispered, remembering how he told me to stay quiet. He just grabbed my hand and when I looked back at him, I noticed his wings were now completely gone. It was as if I was looking at Jerome again, except his shirt was gone. I felt like we were at the gym again and caught myself staring at him. He moved in front of me and led the way while I tried to figure out where the wings had gone that just protruded out of his shoulder blades. Using his other hand, he pulled a piece of plywood that was nailed diagonally against the door off as if it was nothing but a bandaid. The door nearly broke off with the plywood. When he turned the handle, it opened effortlessly, and

I wondered why anyone would think that a single piece of plywood would keep people out.

"No one would think to find us here." His voice was no longer a whisper when we crept inside. I started coughing when I attempted to breathe; choking on the dust that blanketed all the books and other remnants within the old library.

"Wait," I shook my head out of the dreamlike fog it had just been in and refused to go any further unless he answered my questions. He slightly tugged on my arm, but turned towards me again. When he didn't say anything, I continued. "One minute you're Jerome and now you're someone else entirely. How long have you been lying to everyone? And you…"

The lightbulb went on as I realized what had happened.

"They say suspects usually insert themselves into investigations…I was such a fool. You've been involved in the disappearances this whole time?!" I pulled away and began walking out of the abandoned library.

"You can't, they're looking for us," he said.

"Who is looking for us?" I asked, wanting to unload with every question I had at once.

"My brother, but the others aren't too far behind him," he said.

"Others? Who's your brother? Wait. Who are you?" I suddenly realized that the Jerome I had thought I'd known was no longer here. Everything I thought I knew turned out to be a complete lie. I wasn't even sure that I could trust the words that were about to come out of his mouth next.

"Legends that have been passed on for years tell of a god that would walk each human to the other side when it was their time. That god was named Thanatos and was feared deeply for the unknown that he brought people to in their darkest hour…I am Thanatos…or Jerome as you know me"

"And this is my darkest hour, I assume?" I couldn't help but be frank at this point. What did I have to lose? Everyone seemed to be in a trance, like in my dream. Izzy was gone. I had nothing more that could be taken from me.

"Not exactly."

"Care to elaborate?"

"My brother is Hypnos, and that is why people seem to be in a trance-like state. He will put you in a trance or deep sleep. His plan, along with the rest of the gods, was to take our world back."

"Well…I'll tell you right now, the humans don't stand a chance. So you all can take it."

"Some of us appreciate human civilization and want to keep it as it is." I saw him bite his lip as if he was holding back more.

"Why all of a sudden? I don't remember anyone else being in a trance when I was growing up or any of this weird chaos that has been happening," I continued to question him. He had been walking around the library, pacing back and forth slowly as he spoke to me. Jerome…Thanatos finally stopped pacing and reached out for a book on the shelf. He seemed to know exactly what book it was since he flipped right to the page he wanted and walked to me, handing it over.

"See here?" He pointed at the pictures of Greek god statues on the page. "We were all frozen in place like statues and paraded around the world for everyone to see until the curse finally broke."

"So that's you?" I asked, pointing to the Thanatos statue that I was only able to identify from the caption below it.

"What caused you to become a statue?"

"There's this woman...with long, serpent hair and eyes that could kill. For years and years, she was known as Medusa and was feared by all mortals. But then one day, our mightiest god banished most of us immortals down to Earth. We were cursed with human mortality in a way that led us to become victims of Medusa's wrath. One day, she began disguising herself by concealing her deadly locks of hair so we wouldn't know it was her until it was too late. When she unveiled who she truly was…"

"You turned to stone?" I finished his sentence, seeing how hard it was for him to talk about it.

He nodded.

"Why would your mightiest God do that to you all?" I couldn't seem to put the pieces of the puzzle together.

"One of us had fallen in love with a mortal on Earth despite it being against our god's laws. When he found out, he banished most of us…even if we had nothing to do with it."

"Who fell in love with a human?" Words that I never knew would've come out of my mouth just surfaced and I felt like I was dreaming an impossible, unending nightmare.

"That's a story for another time." He wouldn't look at me straight in the face.

"Where do your wings go?" I decided to ask another question.

"We can appear as mortals if we want to fit in. The human world could not handle it if they knew we walked amongst them. And even if they managed to cage one of us, they would just poke and prod at us like a lab specimen…"

"Oh, I know. *I* can barely handle it." I admitted.

He walked over to me after pacing around for quite some time and took my chin in his hand, looking straight into my eyes. I felt like he was looking into my soul; those ocean blue eyes beaming through.

"It wasn't supposed to go like this. There is so much more to say, but we don't have time." He gently released my chin from his grip and I felt like I could just about fall forward, face splat on the floor before me.

He walked away from me and began ascending the steps. I followed, dumbfounded. What did we not have much time for? I thought of my parents and how their bodies were so frozen. Wondering why I wasn't like that too, I wished I could go back to them and make things right again.

"We have to save your kind before it's too late."

HISTORY

19

Although this had been an abandoned library, the upper level told a different story. A king-sized bed was at the edge of the room, mostly concealed in a large fur blanket. Similar to the library, the walls were lined with shelves that contained books of all different sizes and sorts. One shelf towards the bottom had been wiped completely from anything it may have held previously. Before the bed, there was a small desk that had several crumpled pieces of paper folded up as if each one was a foiled plan.

"You've been living here?" I had to ask.

"Well, I come here from time to time...but yeah, I guess so," he answered.

"What is up here that we had to come see?" With any other man, I would have been hesitant on being alone in a room with them. Although I didn't have much choice in the matter, I couldn't help but feel safe despite everything. I wished I could just sit at that desk and write all my questions out for him, but knew he was pressed for time. We...were pressed for time.

"I need your help."

"What do you need my help for? You're a god..."

"I have thought over and over about what I could do to put a stop to all of this, but after seeing how headstrong you are with all of your cases...especially this one, I knew I had to include you in. Not to mention..."

"Not to mention what?"

"Do you have any ideas?" He ignored my question and got back to his original point. When I walked around, I carefully glanced at the vintage bindings of the books. Most of them appeared to be in Greek.

"I need to know more." I pulled out one book and flipped through its pages. He walked over to me and abruptly closed the book, placing it back on the shelf.

"I'll tell you. Just ask away. But we have to come up with a plan before the next nightfall, because that's all the time we have," he replied.

"And then what?"

"It is very likely that people will no longer be here," he said.

"Ok. Let me start at the beginning. Why did I have dreams about all of this?" I asked, still confused by everything.

"You weren't dreaming," he answered simply.

"What do you mean?!" I put my hands on my hips, aggravated by his simple response.

"Each of those times, I found you and had to sneak you back home after Hypnos put you to sleep."

"But why me?"

He paced around the room a bit, then took a book off the shelf that he seemed to know the exact placement of it. When he walked back my way, he flipped to a page and set it down in my lap. This book was surprisingly not in Greek and I was able to read it. The heading read, Prophecy.

Doomed from the heavens, he disobeyed one of the biggest laws that Zeus had bestowed upon them. He fell in love with the one he was forbidden to be with. Her kind was made up of defenseless, sinful humans that no god should have ever matched with. Banished to live on Earth for all of eternity, he was forced to go on in his life without her, as the mortal soul only lasts so long. The serpents that lurked upon Earth had turned them to stone, cursing them to remain as statues until the curse was broken.

"And??" I didn't seem able to put two and two together.

"Did you read the whole prophecy?" he asked instead of explaining further. I looked back down at the page and continued reading.

The mortal soul is reborn as another being entirely.

I closed the book and looked back at him; he was watching me the whole time I read. I wondered how long he knew of me and had been following me; a shiver crawled down my spine. He backed up a few steps, clearly sensing my fear of what everything actually meant.

"You lost someone you loved. You're the god that fell in love with a human. You're the reason why Zeus banished you to live on Earth for all of eternity."

He nodded and stared down at the ground.

"What does this have to do with me?" I asked. "Wait. You think I am the same person who you had lost?"

"You are."

"How are you so sure?"

"We are like magnets. No matter how hard anyone tries to keep us apart, there is a force that keeps pulling us back together."

I thought of all those times I talked to Izzy about Jerome and how nervous I was to even go up to him. I felt like I was the only one who had a silly crush, but it turned out he must've been watching me this whole time. In a way, it was creepy. But it also felt poetic. Too good to be true. That's how most love like this turned out, anyway.

"Am I the reason your kind is going after humans, then?"

"No. Never think that. It is all me." He took all the blame. I still couldn't help but feel I was partially to blame. If keeping away from each other meant saving everyone else, that would be worth it.

"Why did they take Izzy?" I felt my heart sink as I said her name aloud.

"They mistook her for you. They wanted to take the one I fell in love with."

"What did they do with her?"

He looked down at the ground again, then shook his head.

"Jerome. Tell me!"

"I don't know," he said.

"Hypnos is your brother. Did he take her?" I remembered his name from the Greek mythology books I had studied in college.

"It is possible. He thinks I am on his side with ridding this world of humanity, but he is still after you."

"But why?"

216

"Because. Long ago, the human I fell in love with...he had fallen for her, too. The feelings weren't reciprocated back to him, though. He took that rejection very hard and never forgave it. He won't ever allow me to be with you."

I trudged over to the bed and felt my body give out as I sat down and put my head in my hands. A headache was already coming, I could feel it. When I felt the tears stream down my cheeks, Jerome gently took my hands in his own and lifted me up, pressing his chest against mine. He held me close to him and said no words, because there were no words to say. The guilt that overcame me was paralyzing in itself. I might as well have been back in the church when I couldn't move anywhere. I was helpless then, and I still am.

I looked up at him, wiping my tears with my sleeve. His soft, ocean eyes made me want to jump right into them and just escape to the serenity they caused me to feel just by the look. I reached up and hugged my arms around his neck, not breaking eye contact for a moment.

When I rested my head on his shoulder, wishing I could just go to sleep, I felt a shock run through my body. His lips slowly met my neck. Each time he moved away to breathe, I yearned for them to be on my skin again and never leave. I put my head back, allowing him to kiss more of me and let out a moan, enjoying every second of it. All the worries seemed to wash away in an instant to the back of my mind. I backed up to the bed until my legs touched the soft fur blanket and I sat down, my head spinning in pleasure. I shimmied myself onto the bed until I was laying down on it in the middle. He followed my lead, but remained on top of me, continuing to kiss my neck. I unbuttoned my coat and slipped it off the bed. His lips kissed my collarbones and trailed down, gently touching my chest and kissing the outside of my shirt. Despite being fully clothed, I still felt completely exposed. When I opened my eyes again, his wings were back out, shrouding around us like a blanket that encapsulated and protected me. I reached up and pulled his face back toward mine, now pressing my own lips into his. Fireworks went off in my mind uncontrollably. I pulled his shirt up and off of him, then pushed him down so he lay flat on the bed, with his wings folded behind him. I returned his kisses, gently pressing my lips against his neck. When he let out a moan, it made me go that much faster. He pushed me back and got on top of me, unable to take it anymore. I shimmied out of my pants and wrapped my legs around him while he quickly took his off and pressed into me, his hand covering my mouth and stifling each scream I let out. When I finally got used to him, I felt like I was in pure ecstasy. It was hard to keep my eyes open, but I longed to stare into his the entire time. I could feel the love, passion and, most of all…uncontrollable craving all at once. It sent me into a lull and the next thing I knew, darkness engulfed everything around me so nothing more remained other than a black abyss that clouded my mind.

DRAINED

20

I stroked my fingers against the soft fur blanket and slowly opened my eyes, feeling as though I had just awakened from a dream. A sleepless dream. When I tried to sit up, I only fell straight back onto the bed. Any energy I had was gone completely. I kept trying and finally was able to push my back up against the headboard to hold me up. The room was empty, but sunlight gradually trickled in through the blinds. What had I just done? Where was Jerome—or should I say Thanatos? I rolled over to my side and reached down to get my coat from the floor, barely pulling my phone out from a pocket. I had no missed calls, but today was a workday. It was already 10 a.m. Was he already at work? Did he leave without me? I decided to call him.

Voicemail.

Hanging up, I tried to lift myself up again, only to fall off the bed and onto the floor with a thud. I heard someone come in the room, but couldn't see. I managed to roll under the bed to hide. There was no knowing who it could be. Maybe Hypnos found where we were. Footsteps edged closer until I could see the black shoes poking through. I covered my mouth, desperate not to give the slightest hint of my location to whoever it was. They walked back toward the door, and I let out a sigh of relief.

Just then, the slow pounding against the floor drew closer until I could see the same shoes again. Whoever it was crouched beside the bed and I rolled out from the other side, glancing just once at the man who found the hiding spot that only Jerome—Thanatos told me about. I briefly caught the man's dirty blond hair and thick-rimmed glasses before I raced out the door and a wave of dormancy took hold of me. As soon as I reached the top of the steps, I felt my legs buckle from beneath me while I went tumbling down the stairs. The last thing in my line of sight was Thanatos rushing to the bottom of the steps to catch my fall.

- - - - - - - - - - -

"Brother, I thought you said you were going to take care of her..." the man who I used to know as Lance said with his arms crossed over his chest. I urgently looked around the room for Thanatos and couldn't find him anywhere. Just when I was about to get up from where I sat, I felt the coarse rope as it rubbed against my wrists and ankles.

"I always thought you were sick and twisted!" I blurted out, realizing I couldn't escape. I was tied up like some deranged animal. And just a few minutes prior, I had fallen asleep while going down the stairs. My head was throbbing and the light that trickled in from the windows only made it hurt more.

Lance scoffed and, in the next moment, Thanatos walked out from behind me.

"We can use her." He talked to Lance as if I didn't exist.

"Use me?!" I screamed, but it was no use. Neither of them even turned to acknowledge me.

224

"She'll be bait for tonight," he said. "We'll put her there and it will lure everyone else to the same place. They'll want to find her."

I felt like my head was going to explode in rage. He double-crossed me. For his brother. I should have known. Anything that is too good to be true usually is just that.

"You can't do that," I said through gritted teeth.

"Oh yes, we most certainly can." Lance's words jumped down my throat. They seemed to be done ignoring me. Thanatos gave me a sympathetic look from afar, but I wasn't buying a second of it. Not this time.

"So you don't go by Lance either I'm assuming...?" I asked Lance, finally putting together the pieces of the puzzle. If this was Thantos's brother then it was

Hypnos. I already knew that much, but wanted to buy some time to figure out a plan on how to get out of here. He smiled and walked closer to me while Thanatos just stood there and watched.

"Oh, Thanatos didn't tell you?" He smirked at his brother.

I shrugged my shoulders, and he continued.

"Hypnos," he said simply, as if I should've known exactly what that meant.

"Okay..."

"Okay?! You should be scared." His hands were on his hips, and he was peering down at me like some lab specimen.

"I'm shaking in my boots," I said sarcastically. Thanatos laughed and Hypnos shot him a dirty look.

"If you don't behave, I'll put you right back to sleep. Maybe my brother shouldn't have caught you. It would've been fun to see you just crash down the stairs," he said maliciously.

"I would've been knocked out and wouldn't have had to deal with this ridiculous conversation," I said.

"That's it."

He began ripping the ropes that bound my arms and legs to the chair with minimal effort. As soon as his fingers brushed against my skin, I felt like I was in a daze. He scooped me up in his arms and I felt my body go limp as he carried me outside.

"But we need her to lure everyone else tonight," Thanatos protested.

"She'll be fine...for now," Hypnos assured his brother. I could tell it was a lie.

"We can find another way to lure the others. You're right, brother. It's best to get rid of her." His mood seemed to change. Through heavy eyes, I could see Thanatos as he disappeared from view completely. The look on his face said it all; his smile practically cheered his brother on to do whatever he was about to. The man—god—I thought I had come to know very well in that short time, was gone. He was nothing but a mirage, wearing a mask like most people did until it was too late. Eventually, you would see their true colors no matter what. In your darkest times, that is when they would show who they are.

My eyes sealed over in a sleepy daze, but I struggled to keep them open so I could see what was going on. We had already passed through the downstairs library and were outside in the daylight. When I reluctantly looked back at Hypnos, his dirty blond hair and bushy eyebrows weren't the only things I saw. Large wings, much like Thanatos's, stretched out from behind him. They were similar in size, but the complete opposite in color. The long white feathers bolstered out; giving the false impression that he was an angel. Thanatos was nowhere around anymore; I was surprised he didn't join in for whatever was about to happen.

"It's about time we got rid of you..." Hypnos's hateful tone got under my skin, but what hurt even more was the feeling of betrayal from Thanatos. He was one of the few people I trusted with this case and it turned out, he was in on it the entire time.

When I looked down, we were several feet up from the ground. It appeared smaller and smaller until the abandoned library resembled a dollhouse from below.

"What...are...you...doing?" I could barely get each word out; my breaths were slow and shallow. It was as if I were going in slow motion.

"You poor thing, you must be sleepy. Don't worry, it'll all be over soon. We'll be rid of you," he said as we went up farther and farther, nearly reaching the clouds.

"Why?" was all I could muster up enough strength to say. He looked deep into my brown eyes and I felt like I was in a trance. They were so mesmerizing that I couldn't tear my eyes off his if I tried.

"The world doesn't need your kind any longer. You all are nothing but a nuisance. I have seen the way Thanatos looks at you. He wants me to think he's on my side, but this has happened far too many times. This is not something he can save you from this time." He broke his glare, and it was then that I felt released from his imprisoning shackles even if they were just in my mind.

MEANT TO BE

21

"What do you mean?" was all I could ask, finally getting a grip back on reality, although it felt like a never-ending nightmare.

"He's in love with you," he scoffed.

"That's foolish. He's a god. Why would he have an interest in me like that?" I was being partially truthful; even though we had chemistry between us, it was more than possible that it was all a game. At this point, I felt like I was as defenseless as a lamb being that my life and the lives of everyone else depended on these superior beings. We didn't stand a chance against them and the one thing that could save humanity was love? It just seemed that it may not end well...I thought about Romeo and Juliet's demise and it confirmed my hesitations on it working out.

"You don't know?" he asked, a confused look covered his face. "Every hundred years, a woman with scarlet hair finds herself in our lives and makes my brother forget who he truly is. That woman is you, and you're like a magnet we just can't get rid of."

"Impossible," I said, pressing my lips together. I just wanted this all to end.

"Have you ever heard of soul mates?" he asked.

"Yes, and there is no such thing."

"Oh, I wish there weren't a such thing; that would have saved so much time..."

"So you're saying you've met me before?" I confirmed.

"Unfortunately, yes... You're like a curse that just keeps coming back," he said through gritted teeth.

"So what are you going to do with me, then? And how am I awake all of a sudden?"

"I can make you fall asleep with one blink of my eyes or the simple touch of my hand on yours if I want you to. Whatever I want you to do, I can make it happen...just by my gaze into yours." He looked down at the water below us. The corner of his mouth quivered into a smirk and his devilish eyes, no longer hidden behind glasses, stared into my soul.

"Just put me down," I said with little faith he actually would.

"That was my intention, but now I have something even better in mind…"

"And that is?"

"This whole time, I've been so worried about how to get rid of you, but I've been going about it the wrong way."

"You were going to drop me into the waterfall to my death?!" I shrieked so loud it echoed. If it weren't for the continuous rumble from the falls, others would've surely heard me. He wrapped one arm around my waist tighter, pulling me even closer to him and smiled so big I could barely stand it. I tried to look away, but he faced me. If it weren't for my worry about what was going to happen next, I would've closed my eyes to escape the sight of him.

"That was an idea of mine, yes…but this is just so much better." We were still high in the air and all I could hear was the sound of the waterfall as it thundered into watery depths. The only waterfall I knew of was on the very outskirts of town. I had gone there when I was young and could recall that sound in an instant. This time was much different, though, as I feared for my life and very existence.

"What are you going to do?" I asked, unable to break my eyes from his.

"Just keep looking and you'll find out." I felt his gaze take hold of my own to where I couldn't look anywhere else but into his dark eyes; much different from Thanatos's. Despite being heartbroken by his betrayal, part of me longed for the security looking into his eyes gave me. That singular thought faded until I couldn't find it any longer, and my mind was nothing but a blank canvas. Memories escaped me. I was empty. Nothing. The sound of the waterfall was familiar, but any recollection of how I knew it was gone.

FADED MEMORIES

22

I woke up back in my apartment with a killer headache. Even in college, I had never experienced a hangover this intense. I had no idea how I even ended up at home. Toulouse scampered over and rubbed against me repeatedly. I peeked out of the covers at his empty food bowl.

"You could wait one more minute, right Toulouse?" I hid beneath the sheets, wishing I could just go back to sleep and wake up without the migraine I now had.

A small, black nose pushed its way under as he forced himself to join me in the warmth of my bed. I could get a cat to cuddle me, now only if I could manage finding a guy that wanted a relationship and not just a hook-up. The singular thought of finding a guy struck me like there was a piece of the puzzle missing in my mind. It was at the tip of my tongue, but I couldn't place it.

My phone buzzed and broke the silence, scaring both of us up and out of bed. Toulouse shrieked and scratched up my arm on his way to find how to escape the sheets while I clung one hand to the wound that was seeping uncontrollably. I ran over to the bathroom to grab a towel so I could apply pressure to it, not caring about staining one of the few towels I had, knowing full well it would inevitably have to be thrown out. When I walked back to the bed, the root of the problem lay just above my pillow. I grabbed it and checked the messages.

Jerome: It was all an act. Meet me at the station's gym.

I knew of Jerome because we both worked in the same building, but that was it. How he got my number, I had no idea...

Alice: Who are you?

The next text came back almost instantly.

Jerome: What do you mean?

I didn't respond, knowing full well where this would lead if I continued answering. Whatever he thought was all an act…it just sounded like some unnecessary drama that I didn't need. The curiosity in me was tempted to reply to him. The best way out of trouble was to keep myself busy and one way of doing that was by going to work. I flipped the ringer off so my phone wouldn't vibrate any longer and poured some dry food into Toulouse's bowl that would last him a while. Toulouse immediately ran over to me and rubbed against my legs as if to say 'thank you' and I patted him on the head a few times before heading out. A fresh coat of snow blanketed the grounds and glistened underneath the sun's rays. It was still early enough in the morning where the grounds were cold, allowing the snow to remain for longer. As the day continued on, it would likely disappear by the time I got back home.

I thought back to Jerome's text. Something kept pushing me to message him back... I turned my key in the car's ignition, bringing it to life despite the frigid weather. My phone's screen lit up from within my bag and I felt I had no choice but to check it. Another text from Jerome. I didn't understand why he was talking to me out of the blue when I seemed invisible to him my entire time at the station.

Jerome: Alice. Please.

Whatever it was, it was urgent. I pulled out of my spot and headed to work, even though it was my day off and I should've probably figured out a social life of some sort for myself. I was racing toward a man that was a complete stranger to me. My intuition took over while I just wanted to get there. Everything else washed away. As soon as I pulled up, his old car was one of the few taking over a space in the parking lot. The way he texted me made me feel there was something wrong. I pulled around toward the side of the station so my car could remain hidden until I figured out what was going on.

When I walked in the side door, I nearly slipped on the ice right outside the door. Grabbing the handle to rebalance myself, I scanned my badge, and it worked on the very first try. Unlike the usual bustling commotion of the station, it lacked a lot of its staff, and the phone wasn't ringing relentlessly. I cautiously walked through the station from the back, remembering Jerome's text to meet him at the gym. My heart raced as I opened the door that led right there, checking behind my shoulder to ensure no one was watching.

In the main gym room, there was one lone treadmill running with no one on it. There was no sign of anyone in here. I felt like I may be ambushed in some way, but continued on as if I had nothing to truly lose. When I entered the weight room, an indescribable feeling overcame me. Jerome stood by the window, staring outside. He seemed like a watchdog, but I just wasn't sure what he was looking out for. Part of me wanted to walk up to him and press my body into his, but I quickly restrained myself, knowing full well someone like me didn't stand a chance with someone like him.

"You're here," he whispered.

"What's going on?" I refused to whisper back. I didn't care if anyone else heard.

He walked up to me and looked like he was going to put his arm around me. I backed away from the stranger, instantly regretting meeting him in the first place. I always seemed to make the wrong choice...

"Look, I don't know why I even agreed to meet you here, but I don't know you. Coming was a mistake," I said.

He grabbed my hand to stop me, and everything instantly came back to me. The hostage situation we both went to, the various black feathers I found at each crime scene, the abandoned library, and all the nightmares I had where he somehow saved me. I would've fallen back if it weren't for his other hand that pressed against the small of my back. His name slithered into my mind and it was all I could say.

"Thanatos," I whispered, tears forming at the corners of my eyes.

LOST & FOUND

23

Without saying another word, he pulled me to the back of the weight room and opened up a small door we both had to duck in order to get through. All went dark as he reached to close the door behind both of us. We were cramped into the little space and it was impossible not to press myself up to him in an effort to get comfortable again.

"Why are we he—" His finger sealed my lips before I could finish my sentence. I felt his body as I was gently pushed to the very back of this small closet, or whatever it was. He reached into his pocket and handed me a key

I fondly remembered from my dreams. One that felt like it belonged to an antique door from decades and decades ago.

"If I'm not back…think of any place you want to go and turn the key in this door," he whispered.

Before I could ask him anything, he quickly opened the door and was gone. I suddenly felt cold now that I didn't have his presence in the closet with me any longer. I pulled my legs close to my chest and clung to the key, wanting to use it so I could just leave and figure out what was going on. Just when I was about to put the key in the door, I heard a voice coming from the other side. It made me shiver all the more and want to press myself even farther into the closet if I could. His rigid voice made me want to jump out of my skin just thinking about how he dangled my body over the falls and wiped my mind of the case and Jerome. I wasn't sure what his motive was, but somehow Thanatos was able to bring all the memories back. He was able to awaken me again despite my mind being lost and completely in the dark.

"What are you doing here?" Hypnos asked his brother. I could hear heavy weights as they were set down on the ground.

"What does it look like?" Thanatos replied.

"Tonight is the night. We need to prepare," he said. "Or are you missing a little someone...?"

"And who would that be?" Thanatos was acting as if he knew nothing at all. I wondered why he was pretending.

"Oh, you'll see, brother..." Hypnos chuckled.

"What did you do with her?" he barked back like my own personal guard dog. But he knew I was okay. I pressed my ear against the closet door so I could hear more. I felt like a child again when I would try to eavesdrop on my parents' conversations.

"So I guess you do care after all."

"If you hurt her…you are going to wish you were in the underworld already," Thanatos warned.

"Is that a threat?" Hypnos was still joking around.

"You're going to thank me, you know. This girl has gotten in the way of our plans time and time again. Now, she won't even know who you are. She won't even remember a thing you said or did with her."

"I told you, we needed her for tonight." I could almost picture Thanatos as he gritted his teeth together, trying to hold back.

"Don't worry, she'll be there," he said.

My arm slipped and something that felt like a can fell to its side in the closet, causing a metallic cling when it met the floor. They both stopped talking, and I heard the footsteps as they approached where I hid. I quickly pushed the key into the door's keyhole and barely made it in time to turn it as I felt Hypnos turn the handle to open the door. As soon as I turned the key, I squeezed my eyes shut, afraid of what I would find on the other side, but pushed anyway.

Almost immediately, the sound of crashing falls echoed all around me. I pressed my feet into the snow, worried they would meet ice and I'd slip. When I checked behind me, there was no door or any source of where I had just come from. I still clung to the key, wishing I had something like this when I was younger and needed to escape. The many times girls would shut me out of their cliques or poke fun at the glasses I wore would've been much more bearable if I had a way out.

I walked closer to the enticing water despite the cold and dipped one finger in. It would've felt so much nicer to jump right in during the summer. I paced around the very edge, wondering what I should do next. Tonight was supposedly the night they were all waiting for, but what would happen exactly? Was this going to be the last day for humans? Were the gods really that angry with our kind and blamed us for all the wrong that happened in their lives? If what Thanatos said was true, I was partially to blame for being the one that a god fell in love with. When he could have practically anyone else...why choose such an imperfect human? It's something I don't think I would ever understand, let alone the whole reincarnation thing, which I didn't believe for a minute. But then there were actual gods with wings flying about; so if that was true then...

Just faintly over the crashing falls, a familiar voice echoed. I stopped walking and stared out, making sure it wasn't just a ringing in my ear. It was a voice I hadn't heard in a while, but sounded as if it was coming straight from the falls somehow. It turned out to be a song that they were humming. A song that I hadn't heard in ages. The uncertainty of what lay before me caused me to want to run, but there was too much of a risk of falling. I carefully trekked toward the falls and the voice got louder, as did the continuous stream of water. Mist sprawled about and I was so close that drops of water trickled over me, straying from their path down. I pulled the furry hood of my jacket over my head and walked on despite the cold. Behind the falls was a cave I never would've guessed was there if not for the voice that I had no choice but to follow. They must've heard me enter; each step in the cave announced my presence. I pulled my hood closer to my head, worried that bats would swarm out and get mangled and stuck in my hair. There was a dim glow that grew the closer I got to it and when I turned a corner, I found a person sitting with their back to me. Their arms were bound to the chair they sat in and each of their legs restrained in the same way. A furry hood similar to mine hid their identity; I couldn't tell who it was, but knew their voice was familiar. *Was this a trap from Hypnos?*

"I know you heard me," I called to them, refusing to step any closer, just in case.

"Alice?" she said in a low, weak voice. It didn't take anymore for me to realize who she was. I broke through the invisible wall I had set between us and rushed to her side, kneeling down and practically throwing myself at her mercy.

"Izzy!!! Oh my god!!!" I screamed.

"Shh, shh, shh!" If she weren't restrained, she would've probably clasped my mouth shut with her hands. I looked up at her innocently and wanted to share everything that had happened, not knowing if she would even believe a word I said. I felt like I was in a dream; how could she really be here? After all this time? Her long blonde hair looked like it hadn't been washed in days and days; twigs and grass poked through the strands. Her eyes were bloodshot, like she hadn't slept either in a long time. Dark bags lined her eyes and her skin was pale instead of the rosy, cheerful color I had always known her to have.

"Where have you been?" I changed my tone to a whisper.

"I don't even know where to start." It was as if every word took the life out of her. If the chair weren't here holding her upright, she would've likely fallen down.

I started loosening the restraints that bound her and winced at the red marks the ropes made on her wrists and ankles.

"At the beginning?"

SECRET

24

"Wait, so tell me again how you found out that Lance was Hypnos," I said. We were both sitting against the edge of the cave's wall. She could barely keep herself upright because of the little energy she had, but she agreed to tell me everything. Every time I talked, she took time to eat the package of mini muffins I found hidden at the bottom of my bag. They were smooshed down to flattened pancakes, but she didn't look like she cared much at all. I wondered when the last time she ate was.

"He was the guy I was seeing. Remember, the one I kept secret from you?" she said.

"I KNEW SOMETHING WAS WEIRD ABOUT THAT!" I blurted out, but immediately quieted down.

"Shh! You know, they can come back any second... If they find you here with me, you will end up just like me," she said.

"I thought you said he liked you. Why would he do this to you?" I couldn't leave just yet and I was most definitely not leaving without her.

"I don't know. He said something about hating all humans and wanting to banish the world of our existence. There was this girl...he really liked a girl who ended up falling for his brother instead," she said.

"What!" I whisper-screamed. "His brother fell for me though, so is this all my fault??"

"Yep, I guess so. Thanks a lot Alice." She was. half-joking, but we both knew the truth. I was partly to blame. Although, it wasn't my fault that both brothers had a rivalry over me. I would've slapped her on the back of the head if she wasn't in such a fragile state.

"We've gotta get you out of here."

"And then what?"

"I don't know. Find a way to stop them?" I couldn't come up with any good ideas; especially being that they were gods after all.

"What was the last thing that happened between you and Hypnos?" she asked. My mind went back to this very place; the waterfall.

"I think he wiped my memory or tried to at least because one second I was holding on to life by a thread, dangling over the falls as he threatened to throw me

261

down into them from way up high... Then the next second, he said he had an even better plan and I woke up in bed."

"The last time he came into the cave, he told me about how he planned to wipe your memory of Thanatos and make you fall for him instead. He said this would be the perfect payback and destroy his brother's heart just like his had been broken."

"Hm...how does he even think I would fall in love with him? You can't force love," I muttered.

"A conceited god probably believes they can do anything. Does he know you have your memories back? How did you get them back, anyway?" She asked questions that were lingering in my own mind. I missed my best friend.

"It happened when I met Thanatos again. I got a text from him as Jerome. Oh, by the way, Jerome is Thanatos...and I didn't remember who he even was, but he told me to meet him. As soon as I touched him, everything came back. I don't know if Hypnos found out I have my memories back though...the last I heard of him, I was hiding in a closet and then I used this key to get out of there before he could find me."

"Wait!" She had an idea, but was trying to figure out how to put it into words to tell me. I let her think for a moment and grabbed another bag of muffins to give to her. "Okay, if Hypnos doesn't know you have your memories back...now that you know his plan, you can outsmart him. You're not going to like my idea, though."

"Just tell me, it can't be worse than what's going on right now."

"You're going to have to..." She had already chomped down on half the muffins in the bag. I grabbed my water bottle and gave it to her. The anticipation was killing me. "Pretend that you like him."

"NO!" I practically screamed again. How could I even act remotely interested in such a savage beast that wanted to bring nothing but pain to the people I loved?

"You have to. It might be the only way," she said. As soon as she finished the muffins, she tucked the trash away in my bag and handed me the ropes that bound her to the chair.

"What do you want me to do with these?" I asked, confused.

"You need to leave me the way you found me so that he doesn't know."

"No, Izzy. I can't do that." I refused to take them, instead letting them fall to the ground. She grabbed onto both my hands and a shock went through me at how bony her fingers had become. She wanted me to leave her here for dead, so I could potentially do something that may not even have a good ending?

"Either way, the end of the world may be closer than we actually think. But if you could at least try to save us, isn't that worth it? I would be dead no matter what. But knowing I could actually help others live is enough for me."

"You're going to make me cry. Why can't we just switch places? You are going to catch pneumonia if you stay here in this cold cave any longer. It took me so long to find you again and now you're asking me to abandon you? You've been like a sister to me for longer than I can remember."

"This isn't goodbye; things will work out," she said, handing me the ropes again.

"How are you going to get out of here, then? What if he never comes back for you?" Deep down, I knew she was right. This seemed to be the only way. If I left with her, then he would definitely know I had my memories back and I wouldn't be able to fool him.

"Then you'll come back and get me," she said, reassuringly. Both she and I knew there was a good chance we wouldn't see one another again after this moment. I had to do something more. I reached in my pocket and pulled out the key that had brought me here in the first place. When I handed it to her, she instantly took it and started analyzing it.

"Put this in your pocket. If you are able to escape, go up to a wall and a door will appear. Use this and it will take you anywhere you want. Think of someplace he would've never thought you would go. Someplace even he doesn't know about."

"Okay. Deal," she said. "I'm not even going to bother asking any questions because it seems that anything I thought was impossible is now a complete reality." We both laughed nervously; knowing I had to leave soon.

I reluctantly took the ropes and bound her ankles and wrists to the chair again. I tried to make it looser so they didn't irritate the already red skin she had. Knowing she wouldn't be able to return it, I wrapped my arms around her in a hug. I felt like I could break her like a toothpick if I squeezed her any tighter.

"We're going to get you out of here, okay? Just a little longer. Hold on and we'll be getting guacamole and chips at our favorite Mexican place, sipping margs, in no time." I tried to leave her with one of the most positive memories I had before she vanished. It was so terrifying how someone could be there one day and just simply gone into thin air the next. I wasn't going to let it happen again. I would do whatever it took to right this. And now it was more of a possibility. This whole time, he had been several steps ahead of me. But now, things were different.

SACRIFICE

25

Sacrifice. It was something we all had to do at some point in our lives. Some of us would find ourselves in that position more than others. When it came time to choose; that's when a person's true colors would show. To be breaths away from the comfort of a warm home and unlimited food and pass that up, just so that others can survive, was one of the most selfless acts someone could do. Yet we all took those things for granted. Not having to live without warmth or food; most of us take them as rights, when in the end, everything we have is a privilege.

It took everything in me to walk away from that cave and just leave Izzy there like some caged animal, awaiting the predator to come back and eat her whole. Knowing I was going to come face to face with this predator at some point made me worry about how I was going to keep my composure. Even without being in front of him, I wanted to scream just at the very thought of his existence and what he has done. The havoc he's wreaked on this town and my loved ones was unfathomable.

The waterfall wasn't close by, so the trek back home took forever. As soon as I climbed up the hill nearby and found the main road, I called for a cab so I could get to where I needed. Halfway through, I decided not to go back home, but to the station. The sun was already beginning its descent in the sky and I had limited time to ensure my plan went accordingly. I still wasn't sure if Hypnos saw me in that closet before I turned the key. I hoped Thanatos found a way to cover for me somehow. Maybe he could've blamed it on a rodent in the closet...who knows? But they definitely heard the metal can that fell. Stupid metal can...

The cab driver attempted to make small talk, but I was in no mood at all. Every word out of my mouth felt jittery and shaky, as if I had just drank five Red Bulls or taken a bunch of espresso shots.

"You okay back there?" she asked, eyeing me in her rearview mirror. From what I could see, she had long black hair that somewhat resembled Elvira if not for the streaks of violet woven throughout. Multiple piercings lined her ears and when she turned, her pale skin contrasted greatly with the darkness of her hair.

"Never been better." I clung to the door, ready to leave as soon as we got into the parking lot.

"Whatever's going on, it's going to be okay. Just take one thing at a time," she shared her words of wisdom to me. Who was this??

"How is it going to be okay? Humanity as we know it may come to an end tonight and I had to abandon my best friend all because two brothers are having a rivalry over...me? Now tell me, how in God's green Earth are things going to work out?" I blurted everything out all at once and felt like a crazy person saying it all. But a weight lifted off my chest after sharing everything despite it being with a complete stranger.

"Are you sure we're headed to the right place? I think there's an institution right down the road," she joked. Part of me felt like she wasn't completely joking, though. After all, I just basically flipped out on her after she was just trying to say comforting words to me.

"Just drop me off here, okay?" We approached the station and as she slowed down the car, I was already opening the door to get out.

"Well, if you need a lift to the institution, I'm your girl..." she said, laughing away. I pitied her and how naïve she was. She had no idea I was telling the truth. She probably thought I was drunk, but what was wrong with her to act so calm and collected after I pretty much had a nervous breakdown in her backseat?

I sighed, grabbing my bag from the back and leaving the money on my seat. I had bigger problems to deal with and needed to get on with my plan already. When I walked into the station, it was a similar ghost town to what it had been earlier. In the main lobby, there were a few people chatting on their phones. I scanned my badge to get back to my desk. It took a few tries and my patience was already at an all-time low. When I walked through, Lance wasn't at his desk. Most of the tables were unclaimed, and it appeared like whoever was working left in a bit of a hurry. Purses, satchels, and laptop bags were right where people had left them. If they went home for the day, they wouldn't have just forgotten their bags like that at work. I walked on and set my bag to the side of my desk. There was a sticky note waiting for me and the handwriting on it was unrecognizable. The swooping cursive letters were carefully crafted.

I'm onto you. -H

H? Hypnos? Did he already know I got my memories back then? The goosebumps crawled up my spine, and I felt someone standing over me. When I turned, I instantly locked eyes with him. I was thankful for the chair that grounded me, or my knees would have surely buckled. I had no choice but to continue on with my plan. If he was truly onto me, then he would call me out on it, but I could try pretending I don't know what he's talking about.

"Lance?" I said, acting dumbfounded. "Do you know where everyone went?"

He backed away from me; his eyebrows furrowed, confused. This was good. It meant I had a chance.

"What?" he asked, running his fingers through his dirty blond hair.

"The station is pretty much empty; no one takes days off here. Where is everyone? Also…someone left a creepy note on my desk." I picked it up and handed it to him. He took it and glossed over it quickly; we both knew what it said without having to read it again. He bit his lip, nearly causing it to bleed. I couldn't help but bite the inside of my cheek nervously, hoping my plan was working.

"I don't know. I'm just as confused as you, honestly," he said, looking back up at me. "This note is most likely nothing, though. You might as well toss it." When he said the word 'honestly,' it nearly made me crack up right then and there, but I had to keep my head in the game. Everything was on the line.

"Well, we need to find out where everyone went...right?" I said, trying to think of how I could make a move on him for stage two of the plan.

"How do you suppose we do that?"

"I mean, I guess it's nice having the place to ourselves...but still."

"Hmm...come to think of it, that's true," he said as he smiled. He probably felt like his plan was working, too. I bet he just couldn't wait to rub it in Thanatos's face. That would break his heart, though.

"I don't know how I never noticed you before." I took off his thick-rimmed glasses and set them down on my desk, pretending I wanted to stare into his eyes. I had to bury the feeling of wanting to vomit all over the place. This is for you, Izzy. This is for you.

"Well, I guess my desk is behind yours…" He was so bad at flirting, it wasn't even funny.

I sat up on my desk and reached out to pull his body closer to me. He leaned down and pressed his lips into mine; there was no spark like I felt with Thanatos, but it still managed to make my heart stop for a split second. When I opened my eyes again, Thanatos was standing on the other side of the room, and he caught the entire kiss between us. He put his hand to his heart and I could feel his pain from across the room. I wanted to tell him everything, but I couldn't. Instead, I did the exact opposite and continued kissing Lance again and again. No matter what, I needed to make sure this plan worked. Even if it meant hurting the love of my life.

THE PLAN

26

"What's going on?" Thanatos stayed as far away from us as he could.

"Oh, I didn't plan on seeing you here." Hypnos smiled eerily and it made me wish I could wash my mouth out with soap and water just having kissed those lips.

"Alice?" He ignored his brother and kept his eyes on me, slowly moving closer. I could see the hurt in his eyes. The betrayal. I wished I could tell him.

"Sorry, this isn't something we should be doing at work. I don't know what overcame me." I jumped off my desk and stepped away from Lance.

"Oh darling, no one is even here." Lance wrapped his arm around my waist, pulling me closer to him again.

"You guys are together now?" I could hear the jealousy in his tone.

"I guess so," Lance replied. "Don't you have things to do?"

"Yeah...I just...yeah. I'll catch you later." The guilt felt as though daggers went straight through my chest. I broke his heart. I had managed to completely ruin a god. He left the station without turning back. As soon as he left, I pulled away from Lance again.

"Don't tell me you feel bad for him. He'll have plenty more chances, trust me."

"Feel bad for who? Oh, Jerome? No, I just didn't want to be caught like this at my workplace." The lies fell off my tongue as easily as water trickled down from that waterfall. I wasn't normally good at lying, but when it came to saving others, it didn't even matter. The guilt subsided, knowing that it may be worth it in the end.

"The station isn't very busy; I'm sure no one will notice if you head home. You should get ready because I'm bringing you on a date tonight," Lance said, grabbing the sticky notes from my desk and wrote something really quick then folded it before I could read it. "Be there at seven."

He gently slipped the paper into my bag and headed off in the same direction Thanatos had left. As soon as I opened up the sticky note from my bag, I realized the handwriting was an exact match to the threat I had received on my desk before. Sweat trickled down my temples. This was a very dangerous game I was playing. Before, he thought I was going against him and got my memories back. Whatever I did here seemed to work, at least for the time being. I followed the same way he went and as soon as I got outside, expecting to see their cars, they weren't there. Instead, an abandoned parking lot remained, and I realized I would have to call a cab once again. I reluctantly called the cab company and the same driver rolled up in her cab.

"Wow, that was fast," she said. I rolled my eyes and got into the back.

"Can you just bring me home?" I leaned my head against the window and felt like I could fall right to sleep.

"It's going to get better, sweet." She talked to me like a grandmother would talk down to their grandchild, but what didn't make sense was that she was just about the same age as me.

"Who are you?" I finally asked. I could see her eyes as they met mine in the rearview mirror.

"Two truths and a lie."

"Huh?"

"I'll tell you two truths and a lie. It's up to you to decide whether or not I'm being honest." She smiled up at the rearview mirror, then put her eyes back on the road. I had a strange feeling this wasn't a regular cab driver after all. Who did I get in the car with?

"I work for a cab company, I can drive a car, and I know your plan."

"Well, you clearly work for a cab company and drive a car. What plan would you even be talking about?"

"Wrong. I don't work for a cab company!" She laughed. "Oh, this is fun. Let's do another!"

"Fun was not the word I thought of at all. Can't you just tell me your name?" I said through gritted teeth. Why did I even care, anyway? I looked out the window and debated on just opening the door and rolling out. The amount of road rash I'd get would hurt for days if I even survived.

"Boring humans... I'm Eris. Thanatos and Hypnos are my brothers."

"They have a sister?! Wait. Wait. Who are Thanatos and Hypnos?" She caught me in my lies. I was doomed. She would probably go right back to Hypnos to tell him I knew.

"Don't worry; I'm not going to tell him! But geez, Thanatos was quite heartbroken after seeing you two together..."

"How do you know all of this?" I asked, feeling the weight as it sank down in my stomach.

"I'm their sister! Of course I know."

"So you want to see human existence cease too, then..." There was no hope. I wished I at least hadn't broken Thanatos's heart in the process of trying to save everyone. But little did I know I didn't even stand a chance.

"Oh stop. Hypnos is all hurt over how things went between you and Thanatos, but girl...you have him fooled. You have both of them fooled. Hypnos still plans to end everything, but I'm on your side."

"Why?" was all I could muster up enough courage to say.

"Because Hypnos is being selfish and blaming humans for us gods being banished down here when it's really just Zeus's unfair laws. We can't help who we fall for," she said. But was she lying? How did I know if I could trust her?

"I want to believe you, but I don't know why I should bother."

"Listen, you have a chance. I've never seen my brother fall in love with someone over and over again like he did with you. But fooling Hypnos was a good choice because he thinks everything is going according to his plan."

"And what does he plan to do after that?"

"I'm going to guess he invited you to a date tonight? Am I right?" I nodded my head, and she continued, "He's going to have you meet him at the church on Main Street. That's where my other sisters will be, too."

"And then what?"

"He will make everyone you know disappear into a sleepy abyss until the rest of us rid each person of a life one by one. Or that's what he thinks is going to happen anyway…"

"I don't stand a chance."

"When I say this, know that it is coming directly from a goddess's lips. You are the only chance."

DELIVERY

27

Eris came out of nowhere, and I wondered how many other goddesses and gods lived amongst the rest of us. Deceived didn't even come close to naming how I felt. From what she had said, she seemed to be on my side, but believing her would mean I was putting my faith in a complete stranger. Before she dropped me off at home, she gave me a vial and said to use it on Hypnos when the time came. I tried asking what it contained, but before I knew it, she was long gone in her cab. A distant memory, just as everything and everyone else was becoming.

The one thing I was looking forward to most after stepping one foot in the door was already brushing up against the side of my leg. I plopped my bag down and kneeled closer to Toulouse. He continued rubbing against my arm and at one point was on his hind legs each time I rubbed his head.

"Oh Toulouse... I don't even know where to start." I sat crisscross on the floor and let him jump into my lap. "This is the night and everyone is counting on me."

"Meow?" If only he could actually speak. A knock on the door startled both of us. He ran to hide under the couch, but slightly peeked his head out. I tiptoed to the curtain beside the front door and looked out, trying not to be seen by whoever was there. Whoever knocked was gone; the front steps remained unoccupied as if nothing had happened.

"Did you hear that, Toulouse, or was it just me?" I asked him. He pushed further back so I couldn't even see him any longer under the couch. Typical Toulouse. When I slowly opened the door, a black rectangular box sat on the top step. It had a small red tag attached to the top with my name on it. I took it right away and closed and locked the door. Toulouse cautiously stepped forward and patted the tag back and forth that displayed the notorious cursive handwriting I had already grown to hate.

As soon as I opened it up, red tissue paper flowed out and I could tell Toulouse was tempted to play with that too. I quickly moved it aside to find a silk black dress hidden beneath. Under the dress was a folded up note on a red card similar to the tag on top of the box. I pulled it out and winced at the handwriting.

Alice,

Here's something to wear on our date tonight. See you

at 7.

-Lance

The fact that he was still using his fake name instead of who he truly was—Hypnos—was a bit of a relief. It meant I still held the upper hand. At the same time, it was even more of a weight on my shoulders to not mess anything up any further. I rolled my eyes at the dress. It could be seen as a romantic gesture, but from someone I barely knew…it was a bit controlling. He had to pick out what I wore tonight? What nerve.

I reluctantly walked in front of the mirror and peeled off the clothes I had been in for what seemed like longer than a day. A shower would definitely help to wake me up. I left my clothes in a pile beside the elegant dress and stepped into the shower, letting its warmth trickle down onto me as I tilted my head back. I touched my neck and wished for Thanatos to be here again. He made me feel so safe and for some reason, I knew I could trust him without question. Thinking back to when his lips pressed against my neck, I felt worried I'd never be able to relive that again. I had to go see Mom and Dad before whatever was about to happen tonight happened. I don't know how I would keep any of this from them, but I needed to see them. The last time I was there, they had both been in a trance and unable to answer the door for me despite my screams. I doubt they had any recollection of what happened.

Just as I was about to turn off the water to the shower, I heard the bathroom door as it slowly shut. I stayed in the shower and reached an arm out to grab a towel. I may have been overly paranoid, but there was no way Toulouse would close a door like that. At least he hadn't ever before. There was someone in the bathroom with me.

"Whoever is in here, this is not funny. You're a perv!" I screamed. I wrapped the towel around myself and squeezed my hair out, although it was still soaking wet, and peeked my head out of the shower curtain; allowing the rest of the curtain to conceal my body from view. Thanatos leaned against the sink with his arms crossed. I must've been under the hot water for a while because the steam still lingered in the air. The added tension between us didn't help.

"I'm sorry, I needed to come here to ask why," he slowly said.

"And you couldn't wait till I at least got out of the shower?!" I pulled the curtain to the side and stepped out, allowing my feet to press into the foam mat on the floor.

"We're running out of time…"

"Look, I don't know you. We just work together, but this is creepy. This may actually be stalker status right here." I remembered my duty to save Izzy and everyone else. I needed to continue on with the lie, no matter how heartbreaking it was for either of us. Someone could've been listening to our conversation and that would've ruined everything.

"I don't understand. He wiped your memory again?" he asked, persistent. Why wasn't he giving up? I could see the hurt in his eyes.

"Who? Wiped my memory? What are you even talking about?" If someone was listening in, they couldn't see exactly what was going on... I just had to worry about what they heard.

"Alice, I thought we were together." He looked straight into my eyes, pleading like a dog would for its most precious toy.

"Why would we be?" I put my finger over my lips as if to shush him and took his hands in mine. "I don't even know you." When I thought it couldn't get any hotter, the closer our bodies got, the more hot flashes I felt.

"Because we're meant to be," he continued staring, confused. His head tilted slightly, as if he were trying to figure me out.

"You and I? No. I'm with Lance." When the words rolled off my tongue, I felt like I had not only put a dagger through his heart but also my own. I needed to show him I really felt otherwise. I pressed my body into his, water still running down my arms and legs from the shower.

"But why?" His head tilted the other way as I got even closer to him until there was no space left between us.

"I...love him." I wasn't talking about Lance, though, anymore. In my mind, I was talking about the man right in front of me. The dark angel who somehow showed me the light through all the pain. The gym rat, who I didn't listen to for a second while he was trying to teach me workouts, but instead just watched him in awe. The god that was too good to be true.

"Oh..." his ocean blue eyes left mine and not even a second had passed until I missed them. I felt his persistence fade and knew it wouldn't be long before he left.

"So much..." I added, taking his chin in my hand and pressing my lips into his. The weight that had found itself in the bottom of my chest now grew wings as it leapt to the top. I bit his bottom lip and pulled up, wanting to get even closer to him, but we were already as close as could be. He pulled away and I could see his jaws clench again and again as if he was holding back from doing so much more.

"Him?" he asked, confirming what I had said.

"I love him more than he will ever know. I would risk anything; I would even risk our love to save him from the evil in this world." It was then that it seemed to click for him. He wrapped his arms around my waist where the towel still clung and kissed me back again and again, barely stopping to gasp for air.

"I know he loves you too and wouldn't give you up for anything in the world."

MEANING

28

Love? What does love mean?

Growing up, I never questioned the love I had for my mom and dad. When we'd go to Grandma and Grandpa's house, I would feel that same love I felt for everyone else in my family. From a young age, I knew I was accepted by all of them. Even with my quirks. Don't get me wrong. We would all butt heads every now and then, but we would always end up coming back together because of that one syllable word. Love.

It wasn't until high school when I began to use the word in a much different way than I ever had before.

I'd have a crush on a guy and the fluttery feeling in my stomach would make me feel like I was in love with him, but in fact...I was only infatuated. Deeply infatuated. But after several not so great breakups, I realized how often we misuse that word when we get older. To love someone is to genuinely care for them, both inside and out. You don't want them to change and you know they have your back just as you have theirs. There is no question of whether or not they like you, because you know. You know from the way they look at you and speak with you. You feel respect and understanding from them, and it has no bounds. There is absolutely no roadblock or obstacle that could come and go unbroken. They will find a way. Both of you will find a way to make your love work. It feels like a fire in your chest that only ignites more and more as time goes on. No matter how dark life can get, that flame shines through and is always there to remind you the world is not so lonely after all.

The people we come to love in life as we grow up shape who we are, but when we go out into the world and find that unbreakable bond with someone else…it's truly unforgettable. There are no ties to that person, but they just form in the matter of seconds.

With Thanatos, I felt that unbreakable bond. From the many times I talked about him to Izzy to the moments where I felt so connected to him that I felt exactly what he felt as if we were one.

It was a relief to know Thanatos was finally on the same page as me and that I wasn't actually breaking his heart after all to follow through with the plan I had. All along, it was one of the most difficult things I ever had to do, to pretend I didn't like him. He must've thought I had a chance because he continued talking about my 'love for Lance' all while knowing it was truly how I felt about him. I said a few more words to him about how much I was 'into Lance...' and he smiled, nodding to acknowledge he knew exactly what I was doing. When he left, I dried and combed my hair, then slipped into the black dress that was sent to me. It hugged every curve of my body. The short sleeves draped off my shoulders and its velvet texture was so soft, but also warm. It went all the way down, just below my knees. When I spun around in front of the mirror, I could definitely see why shallow Lance chose this one. It accentuated my ass. I rolled my eyes, and like clockwork, Toulouse slowly walked over and rubbed against the dress, leaving some cat hair stuck to the bottom. This was why dark clothes didn't mesh well with me... Toulouse's hair always found a way to cling to whatever I had and I'd have to carry around a lint brush just to keep it looking clean. I shook my head and walked into the living room, checking the time. It was only 6:00 which left me some time to stop at my parents' house.

"Toulouse..." I said as I put my coat on, buttoning it all the way up so I didn't have to deal with Dad's reaction to my dress. There would be too many questions. "I'm going. If I am not back...you know where your cat food is."

Kneeling down, I kissed him on the forehead, wishing I didn't have to go. I honestly didn't know if I would ever see him again. I had to just keep reassuring myself that I would, though, because I couldn't go into this without that hope.

Goosebumps crept down my spine as soon as I walked outside to my car. Although I was able to put on my long black boots with the dress, it still wasn't nearly warm enough for the winters we had in New England. When I got in, I cranked the heat as high as it would go and dialed Mom because Dad was likely watching his silly YouTube videos on his phone as usual.

"Hello?" Her voice was reassuring and upbeat.

"Hey, I'm going to stop by real quick to say hi," I said. What other excuse did I have?

"Huh? Since when do you do that? Why don't you stay for dinner?" she asked.

"Umm, I already ate. I just miss you guys." I felt a tear form at the corner of my eye, but I pressed it quickly so it wouldn't smudge my mascara.

"Okay then, whatever you say..." she trailed off, talking about the groceries she just picked up and how she would never let Dad grocery shop again because of all the Twinkies, Snoballs, and other 'junk food' he would get. She actually talked so much that I could've hung up and she would've still been going on. I was already pulling into the driveway when she finally paused for a moment to see if I was still there.

"I'm actually already in your driveway! I'll see you in a sec." I hung up as she was telling me I better not have sped all the way there.

"Look who it is!!!" Dad was already at the door and opened up his arms wide to hug me. "Woah, woah, woah... You're all dressed up, aren't you?!"

"What?! How do you even know that?" I asked, looking down at the very end of the dress that poked out from below my jacket.

"I'm your dad. I know everything."

"Well, maybe not everything..." I attempted at changing the subject.

"So, who are you going on a date with?" When he asked, I wanted to gush about Thanatos...but remembered at the last second to continue talking about Lance.

"Just a guy from work."

"Come on, you didn't tell us about anyone!" he said, leading me into the tv room. Mom was sitting on the couch eating a bowl of cereal.

"Isn't it a little late to be eating cereal?" I asked.

"What? I wanted a snack," she said with a mouth full of Golden Grahams.

I laughed and wished I still lived with them sometimes.

"Alice met a guy," Dad informed her. I rolled my eyes. Now the whole town was bound to know. Well...in a few hours, it wouldn't even matter, anyway.

"Oh yeah? Tell us about him." She sounded normal now that she ate and swallowed the mouthful of cereal she had.

"There's not much to say; it just all happened so fast I guess."

"Well, he better slow down unless he wants to have a firm talking to." Dad crossed his arms over his chest. If only he could be strong enough to take on Lance... He would stand no chance, though.

"Oh, calm down. We're just going to dinner."

"So you *haven't* already eaten?" Mom asked, calling me out.

"I mean, I ate a little bit before..." If you count the pastry I had for breakfast like...more than ten hours ago.

"So, where are you going to go?" she asked.

"It's a surprise."

"Well, be sure to send me your location as soon as you get there, just in case something happens. Bring your pepper spray with you. You never know people." I looked over at Dad as he was already checking my bag to make sure I was carrying the pepper spray they got me for my birthday.

"It's here. She's all set," he confirmed. Geez, what a duo.

"Come on guys, I'm going to be fine! I've actually gotta get going before I'm late."

"I'll walk you to the door." Dad handed my bag to me. He ended up walking me all the way to my car door and hugged me like he would never see me again as he normally would. Except this time, it might be the very last time.

"You're smart, you know what to do. I trust you, I just don't trust whoever this guy is," he said. I wish I could reply, 'Neither do I...' but I needed to reassure him.

"I've known him for a while and we're just going to get some food, that's all. I'll call you when I get home."

"You better."

"I promise!"

"Pinky promise?"

"Pinky promise." I held out my pinky and hoped this wouldn't be the first and last promise I would ever break with my dad.

RESERVATIONS

29

The snow began to trickle down from the sky as soon as I started driving. Although I had the address on the sticky note Hypnos gave me, I knew exactly where to go. After appearing so many countless times in my nightmares, I was finally going to walk directly into the midst of it all to try to save everything I had ever known. Having Thanatos on my side counted for something, but still worried me. If I ended up saving everyone, what would come of Hypnos? I couldn't exactly kill a god. And part of me knew he would stop at nothing. Or would he? Was there something more important to him than his hatred for humans?

As soon as I parked my car, I already heard the familiar harp playing simple, soft notes from within. There wasn't a single car in the parking lot. I put my hood up and ventured out into the night, slowly creeping up each step to the church I had so carefully tried to stay away from. I thought of both of my parents and took a deep breath, praying I would see them again. The wind billowed and caused me to rush through the doors of the church, seeking its warmth. After pulling the colossal door open, it felt almost like a sauna inside. The heat was cranked all the way up, despite the absence of anyone in the parking lot.

In the very back of the church, past all the pews, was an orchestra. I slapped my side to confirm I wasn't dreaming. The musician playing the harp effortlessly continued to play while everyone else remained as still as statues. They were just looking at their own instruments; not at each other, not out at the audience. And the audience...it was as if everyone in town was at this orchestra.

I continued walking down the aisles and looked at each person, trying to see if there was anyone I actually knew here. None of them turned to acknowledge me. Their eyes were glued to the front as if it was a stage instead of an actual church. To my left, Clara sat down beside some of the EMTs that had helped her in the ambulance. I stopped and waved my hand in front of her face. She didn't even blink once. As soon as I turned, Hypnos was directly to my right, watching me the entire time.

"Oh hi, what is going on?" I asked. He took each sleeve off and draped my coat over his arm, checking me out up and down.

"I hope you're not too hungry. We've got a bit of a show to watch."

"I can see that…"

"Come." He wove his arm into mine and led me toward the very front of the church and around the orchestra. The violinists began to chime in. When we passed the harpist, her long, pale fingers were dripping with blood. I wondered how long she had been playing for and winced as I, too, felt her pain.

"Why don't you stop them from playing? It looks like it's hurting them."

"Don't worry about them. Come on." He tugged at me more aggressively. It was clear I was just a meaningless human to him still, despite pretending to take an interest in him. "There's something I've been meaning to show you."

I didn't say any other words, but instead my mind wandered to a million different places. Where was Thanatos and why was Hypnos taking me all the way toward the back? There was a small room I had never entered before, right behind the orchestra. As far as I knew, this was the room where a priest would go so he could prepare for each mass. Dimly lit candles were the only things illuminating our way. It was almost as if he made a candlelit dinner of some sort for our date, but I had a feeling he had other plans in mind. He was still clinging to my side and his arm acted as restraints, ensuring I wouldn't be able to flee.

"How are we going to see each other?" I asked, hearing the fear in my own shaky voice.

"Oh, you will. I told you I have something really great planned for tonight...here, stay here and I'll be right back," he said, finally leaving my side. At first, I could see his feet as he trailed away, but then his entire being disappeared into the distance as he walked away. To my right, I heard a moan like someone was fighting to say something, but I couldn't see them. Light flooded through the room all at once while the candles now remained useless. I jerked my head toward the sound and my heart instantly sank at what lay before me.

BROKEN

30

His thick, black hair was disheveled as sweat seeped down the sides of his face, giving an ethereal glow to his skin. Chains bound his arms behind his back while he knelt down on the ground, his ankles tied back in a similar way. Duct tape was pressed against the soft lips I had grown so fond of. He was facing away from me, but on the other side of him was a woman of olive complexion with a head wrap that concealed all her hair. She had piercing green eyes and was staring intently at me. I rushed to Thanatos's side in an instant without thinking.

"What happened to you? Why are you tied up?" I asked, ignoring the woman completely. When he moaned again in response, I realized how stupid I was to ask questions without even helping him first. Right as I was about to tear the tape off of his face, he shook his head repeatedly. I ripped it off anyway. "I can help you. Why are you shaking your head?"

He continued shaking his head and offered no response.

"Thanatos, who did this to you?" I walked around him to his legs, only to find the chains had a lock on them for a key that I didn't have. When he still offered no response, I knelt down in front of him, blocking the space between him and the woman.

"Silly girl," she laughed menacingly.

"Huh?" I turned toward her instead.

"You somehow managed to make a god fall for a human...and you ask, 'who did this to you?'" She laughed again to herself.

"I'm the silly one, yet you're also chained up?" I turned my back to Thanatos and faced her instead.

"Can't you see the rivalry?"

"What are you talking about, and who are you?"

"She's Medusa..." Thanatos finally spoke. If my heart could've sunk even lower, it just did. I stood up and backed away from both of them, looking back and forth to assess what was going on.

"I am and you lovers have found yourself in a bit of a predicament... for some time now," she said. "And it's getting quite annoying to be used for the same purpose over and over again. I was off enjoying myself and then the next thing I knew, I was here dealing with this stupidity."

I had no sympathy for her. While people were disappearing and others had lost their loved ones, all she seemed to care about was that she was having a good time and was taken away from it?

"So then, why are you even here? Go back to where you came from."

"I was taken," she hissed.

"Why?"

"Hello everyone, it looks like you have all introduced yourselves already. I was hoping to have the pleasure..." I heard Hypnos's voice again as he walked back in.

"Hypnos, you have to help—" I wished I could've taken the words back, but it was too late.

"Oh...so you were pretending all along that you still didn't have your memories? How did you even get them back then?" He caught me in my lie.

"Look, I don't know what you're doing, but it needs to stop. It's foolish."

"Alice..." Thanatos looked down at the floor as he whispered my name, "just go."

I couldn't help but to run to his side and now that Hypnos knew everything, I had to comfort him. It was like a magnet was pulling me toward him. Always. And no matter what I or anyone else did, I would never be able to stop its pull. I had no intention of wanting to, anyway. I hugged my arms around him and the warmth I had once felt in his embrace was now gone. All that remained was dull and emotionless.

My arm was tugged off of him while Thanatos's eyes bulged, unable to do anything to stop his brother. Hypnos yanked my arm to follow him and brought me over to a chair, pushing me down. He crouched so he could look straight in my eyes. When I wanted to continue looking at Thanatos, I now no longer had control over where I was even looking.

"That's good. Look right at me." His voice sent my mind into the clouds. I felt light-headed and weak, but couldn't even blink for a moment. His eyes imprisoned me in an unending daze. "You will look at your lover and not take your eyes off him, no matter how painful it gets."

My gaze quickly shifted from Hypnos to Thanatos while he walked away from me and toward Medusa. Seeing him so powerless and in pain hurt me to my core. It was even worse that I couldn't do anything to help him. I had to sit here and watch whatever was about to happen.

"Why don't you just get on with it?" Medusa growled. Whatever was about to happen was something she clearly didn't want to be a part of, either.

"I can leave you tied up forever; watch what you say." Hypnos barked back at her.

"Hm…" Medusa said, and I could hear the smile in her voice. I hoped she had a plan or was on our side at the very least.

"Alice, Alice, Alice… I tried to save you, but you got in your own way. We could have been together…then you choose my brother repeatedly. You led me on, only to deceive me. That's all humans do is deceive one another…"

"You don't know what you're talking about," I interrupted him while I still stared straight at Thanatos, who cowered down on the ground.

"And so humans," he ignored me, "do not deserve a beautiful world like this that they destroy anyway with their awful habits. One of my favorite things is how they will pay to kill themselves through all the chemicals and toxins they blindly purchase. You all are so naïve." He walked over to me, blocking my view of Thanatos, and gently took my chin in his hands. "But you, Alice, you were different from the rest of them. You have only ever been out to help others until you decided to deceive me."

"What did I do to lead you on?! Go to work?!" I couldn't help but blurt it out. He was making me so angry and the fact he had all the control made it even worse.

"You're oblivious too, aren't you? Well, that's typical of your kind, so I wouldn't expect any less."

"Well, I'm sorry if I did something to lead you on, but you can't choose who you love and that's just what happened," I said, looking at Thanatos again when he finally moved out of my view.

"Why would you lie, though?" he asked. "Did you two make this plan together? You must've."

"She did nothing. It was all my idea," Thanatos finally broke his silence without even picking his head up to face either of us. Hypnos jerked back to face his brother.

"Don't cover for her. It's a shame you must suffer for a stupid human, but this is the only thing that will hurt her most and I need to hurt her like her kind has hurt us." He walked around to Medusa and pressed his hand on her head wrap. In the corner of my eye, I noticed something was moving beneath the wrap.

Hypnos jumped back and yelped while Medusa laughed. He turned the opposite way of her and held his finger that had just been bitten close to his chest.

"Can't you keep them under control?" he asked her.

"Not when I am threatened. You better be careful or the same fate will come of you as your brother." I couldn't understand why Hypnos wasn't facing Medusa, but then remembered the prophecy in the book at the abandoned library.

The serpents that lurked upon Earth had turned them to stone, cursing them to remain as statues until the curse was broken.

SAVIOR

31

All at once, the lights went out and hissing serpents were released from their hold. I yearned to run to Thanatos's side, but remained glued to the wooden chair Hypnos bound me to. When the lights came back on, the piercing scream came so fast, I couldn't cover my ears in time...but felt someone's hands clasp over my eyes so I couldn't see what was going on.

"It's going to be okay, trust me," a familiar voice whispered. Wailing filled the air before us and it wouldn't stop. I could tell it was Medusa; her once sarcastic tone was now drowned in her own tears.

"Don't touch me!" she screamed.

"Just a minute," Eris said.

"You have no idea what you're even doing..." Medusa cried out, "just unbind me."

Eris must've done as directed, because there were no more complaints. I could hear the chains fall to the ground.

"She's fine now. Take your hands off her eyes," she gave another direction.

Several dead snakes fell to the ground and what once stood beside Medusa was now a towering statue that resembled Hypnos. He was facing her and wielding a sword in his right hand that I guessed he must've chopped off some of her hair with. Medusa's head wrap concealed the remaining snakes that were spared from his sword. Being able to blink showed me Hypnos's curse had broken as there was no more music playing from the main stage. I felt a relief for the musicians whose hands were bloody after playing for so long. Eris was kneeling down on the ground, gathering the remnants of the chopped snakes that lay lifeless.

"Don't touch them," Medusa hissed and knelt to take them from her. She kissed each one as if it was a pet of hers and placed them into her bag.

Izzy pulled me up off the chair and I could barely stand; I felt weak in my knees. It was as if I had forgotten how to. I clung onto her for balance. "How are you here?"

"This," she showed me the key. "Right after you left, Hypnos came back to untie me and said I was on my own. I had no idea how I'd make it out of the cave when, all of a sudden, there was a keyhole on a random wall, just like you said would happen. It made no sense, but I tried it and ended up at the station. That's where I met Eris and we came up with the plan."

"But if Hypnos is cursed as a statue...then that must mean that Thanatos is too." I looked down at the ground, not wanting to see him that way. Salty tears streamed down my cheeks and entered my mouth, causing me to taste the same bitterness I felt inside my heart. Warm hands took mine off of my eyes, but I still didn't look. The weakness that I felt in my knees had now spread to my entire body. My fingertips pressed against a rugged beard. I stood up so quickly, I could barely contain myself. His ocean blue eyes seeped into my own. I wanted to jump into them as if they were pools I could stay in and never leave.

"I thought you were—"

He put his finger to my lips to shush me before I could say any more.

"I'm here and I'll always be," he said as he pressed his hand to my chest. "And even when you can't see me, I'll be in here."

I practically jumped into his arms and wrapped my legs around his waist. "But how did your brother turn yet you're okay?"

"He was blindfolded," Medusa chimed in. "You'll have to thank your two sidekicks over here."

I looked over at Izzy, then Eris. Their clever plan was better than anything I had ever been able to come up with all this time while I was trying to investigate the disappearances. And now, all those people...they were in the church in a trance. But, were they still?

"Where is everyone?" I jumped back onto my feet and grabbed Thanatos's hand to lead him back into the main church. When I felt a tug pulling me the other way, I found him as he planted his feet and refused to go any further.

"I can't go in there with you."

"But why not?" I asked. His sister, Eris, walked beside him and answered for him, which I had found she must've been keen on doing.

"Oh, you know…they kind of blame us for this whole thing," she said. "Guilty by association."

"What was your part in it?" I asked, curious. He winced at my question as if he predicted I was going to ask it, but had been dreading it all along.

"Please understand this when I tell you…" he prefaced his answer. "They were brought here to meet their death. After Hypnos put them into a trance where they couldn't leave, I would walk each and every one of them to the next chapter after life."

"But why?" I backed away from him.

"Alice, all humans were thought of as the reason for our curse down to Earth."

"But if I'm to blame, then why are you even here with me? Will you be walking me to my death, too?"

"I thought the same, but after I found you, I realized I was wrong. So very wrong."

"Would you have really killed all of those people?" I asked, hoping he would at least give me his honesty.

"Yes...but I guess that's why they say to be with someone that brings out the best of you. It is you who has saved them...and me. I'm not going to ask for your forgiveness, but go out there and explain what happened however you'd like. They deserve some form of explanation."

I bit my bottom lip, not knowing what else to say. When I looked back up, Eris was already gone, but Izzy remained. She gave me a comforting smile. There was deep worry in Thanatos's soft eyes. I tied my messy hair back and reluctantly walked away from him. I wanted to forgive him for his ways, but he had planned to kill the entire race. I thought back to the man in the apartment building with Clara and how he had supposedly killed himself right beside Thanatos. Was that truly a suicide?

"I'm coming with you," Izzy said. She stood by my side and we walked back into the church. Everyone was standing in a crowd, talking to one another, dumbfounded. They must've had no idea how they even ended up there.

"What do I even say?" I asked her.

"Whatever you feel is right."

As soon as we got to the center-stage where the priest would usually stand, everyone quieted down. They seemed eager to hear.

"We are investigating what has happened, but the perimeter has been checked, and you are all safe and free to go. It is okay," I said, wishing I could explain more, but I didn't know exactly how much they knew.

"What is going on?!" one of them asked. "How do you know anything?"

"I assure you all are safe and sound. You can all head back home, but if there are any clues or evidence you have, please submit it to the station."

"We want more answers!" a man shouted.

"I can assure you, I do too..." I walked off the stage and through the crowd, finding the many people whose case files I had sorted through, thinking they were long gone and dead. Seeing them in person made it all the more real. It seemed like they were directing their anger at me instead of the situation. A bunch of them pushed Izzy away from me and swarmed around me, shouting their questions and blaming me. Their verbal threats turned physical as they repeatedly shoved me this way and that. A woman that looked harmless spit in my face while someone pushed me from behind. I was laying flat down on the ground when several decided to kick me in my sides.

"Stop!" Izzy shouted from just a few steps away. They were leaving her alone, but targeting me for some reason.

"Shut up. She clearly knows more than she's letting on," someone said, and that same person kicked me in my gut. I hugged my knees close to me and lay in the fetal position, defenseless.

"You're going to kill her! Stop! Thanatos! Thanatos!" Izzy called out to him. Darkness crept in and swept me away to another place.

FINDING THE LIGHT

32

I awakened to a shooting pain in both of my sides and stomach. My legs felt limp, and I lay lifeless on the ground. The tiled floor was cold on my hands and face, but it was nothing compared to the gut-wrenching pain I felt everywhere else. Where there had been yelling and screaming before, there was now silence. Beside my hand, there was something soft and delicate. I rubbed my fingertips along it and realized it was just like the many black feathers I found at each of the crime scenes.

"Thanatos?" I asked.

"I'm here. Don't worry, they're not going to get you."

When I peeled my eyes open, I realized his wings were fully extended and shielding me, allowing no openings or light to get in.

"Don't hurt them. They didn't know." I pushed my own pain aside and worried about the naïve people who thought they would take matters into their own hands by taking out their anger on me. They must've thought I had something to do with it.

"They hurt you."

"Just take me away from here. Please."

He effortlessly scooped my body up in his arms and his extended wings acted as a wall behind us as we exited the church. When we got outside, we went straight up into the sky, leaving everything behind.

"Is this a bad time to tell you I'm scared of heights?" I asked.

He laughed. "Even in the worst situation, you are somehow able to find the light in it."

"I don't think this is a very bad situation, being that we are both alive and we've saved just about everyone. I'd say this is a pretty good day." Just as I said 'good,' I felt the pains in my side throbbing again.

"You're going to heal," he said. Instead of soaring over the buildings, we continued going up into the sky.

"You know…I can't breathe if we go up that high."

"It is time we have finally dealt with this once and for all. And you are living proof."

"Where are we going? Shouldn't I rest?" I said to take me away from here, but didn't exactly specify where he should take me. And now he was doing just that, but the destination was a mystery. He ignored me and continued on, a smile stretched across his face. I didn't like being in the dark on things...but then again, I guess I chose the wrong person to be with if I wasn't going to try to get used to that.

A thick white cloud puffed out above our heads; I ducked my head as we went right into it. When we came out from the other side, it was like nothing I had ever seen before. Despite my worries, I was able to breathe...even more clearly than when I was on the ground. A colossal gate somehow stood on the cloud, with many stairs right behind it, leading up to a city of gold on a cloud that was higher up. The gates had gold leaves that wove in and out of each pole, embellishing its entirety in a shimmering tone. When we reached the entrance, there was one man that had larger muscles than any bodybuilder I had seen on Earth. His entire body was toned, and he had light brown hair that extended into a beard. The only thing that clothed him was what appeared to be lion skin wrapped around his waist. His furrowed eyebrows and giant bat with thorns poking out every side made me turn my head into Thanatos's chest, afraid of who we were meeting.

"When you are told that you're banished, what does that mean to you?" The man's voice was rigid and threatening.

"We have been banished down there for centuries, Heracles. I have something that will prove Zeus wrong in his claims about humanity."

"The poor defenseless rabbit lying in your arms?" he asked. Was he referring to me? I was prey in their eyes... Oh, what would come of me...?

"She is much more than one can perceive. This is something he has to see."

"You are a fool to waste his time...go back the way you came and don't come back again." Heracles gave him no chances. Was this how gods and goddesses were to one another? If so, it seemed their world was much more unforgiving than ours.

"I'm not going anywhere."

Just then, Heracles put the big bat behind his head and slowly walked toward both of us. Thanatos set me down behind him. As soon as I touched the cloud, I felt like I was going to fall right through, but didn't. Some other worldly magic kept me from falling to my death.

346

His dark wings were still out; I could barely see Heracles from where I lay. I propped myself up on my forearms, not knowing where else I could possibly go.

"And you're a bigger fool for thinking you could beat the gatekeeper of Olympus and get through on your own."

"I don't need to win. I just need to make a ruckus that will get Zeus's attention."

"Well, in that case..." I heard the bat come down hard and winced, squeezing my eyes shut. When I peeked, I found Thanatos had just managed to dodge it. He walked around to the other side of Heracles to keep him away from me and the beast continued toward him. Even in this moment where he barely stood a chance, Thanatos's skin glowed and radiated warmth from within. Despite the darkness he represented, his light was not something that could go ignored.

The repetition of Heracles whacking his bat down only to miss Thanatos seemed to happen again and again. It was only a matter of time until one of them was hurt, but Thanatos had no weapons of any sort. At least, I didn't think so. I wished he could just take me home instead of being up here where we were not wanted, but realized we weren't wanted anywhere at this point. They had both come full circle and Thanatos was standing to my right. Heracles tricked him by pretending he was about to whack his bat down but instead waited an extra moment and quickly moved to where Thanatos moved. I could see his exact plan and pushed myself forward, so I was standing directly in front of Thanatos. I was in between him and Heracles, who had just struck down with his bat. Instead of hitting Thanatos, I felt the thorns from the bat pierce into my flesh. I couldn't catch a full breath and blood was seeping out all around me. The thick, soft cloud was no longer white and airy. Blood rained down beneath me and the depths of everything I lay on turned dark gray. Heracles and Thanatos both rushed to my side. Neither of them had expected I was going to throw myself in front of him. The once defenseless rabbit they thought I was now turned into a hero that saved a god she had grown to love. Thanatos's ocean blue eyes stared into mine. Tears streamed down his glistening face and dripped onto my body that was red with blood. He took each of my hands in his own and continuously shook his head. The bright skies of Olympus turned into pitch black until only Thanatos and I were left. I looked down at my body and there were no wounds any longer or pain. The pain from before had subsided, along with each thorn that pierced into me. It was as if nothing had ever happened. Thanatos shook his head and looked down.

"It is not supposed to be your time," he said. "I can't bring you there."

"Bring me where? I'm fine now; we can be together."

"You don't understand. Alice. I must guide you now." He sat down in the darkness. His once emanating strength now dwindled down until he lay there, weakened and dull.

"My life is—? I'm—?" I couldn't say the word. "But what if I'm not ready?"

"No one is ever ready when it happens. And neither is anyone around them. Like every other time, you will come back. Remember me in your soul." He pressed his palm to my chest.

A strong wind came and lightning struck, illuminating the darkness that had just encapsulated both of us. We both looked up in shock and fear at what stood before us.

WORTHY

33

Aside from the reoccurring strikes of lightning, there was still no light. Each time, it made me nearly jump out of my skin but also allowed me to see the god that stood before us. His gray and white hair was wavy and pushed back by the gold embellished crown he wore. A similar armor lined up from his feet to both of his knees. On each kneecap, there was a lion's face engraved into the armor. A light blue cloth covered below his torso. His skin was tanned and in his right hand, he held a gold lightning rod. It had to be the god we had gone all the way up to Olympus for. Was I still dead? Was this what death was like? Just as confusing?

"Thanatos," his voice bellowed out like thunder that came before each strike of lightning. It seemed to echo as if we were in an enclosed space.

"Zeus."

"I see you have brought an important matter to Olympus."

"It may be too late."

"Tell me, then. Tell me what you have come to tell me, anyway."

"This girl. This human you have said the gods cannot be with... she has managed to prove herself even more worthy than any god I have seen before. I've come to show you who she is, but I fear it may be too late," Thanatos revealed, looking down at the ground. I could hear the strain in his voice as he attempted to explain his reasoning for coming back to Olympus.

Instead of answering, Zeus walked over to me and took my chin in his colossal hands.

"And out of the selfish beings came this one?" he asked. "I saw."

"What did you see?" I asked, forgetting I was talking to a god for a split second.

"She threw herself in front of you to protect you, someone not even of her own kind."

"And now it is too late. I must walk her to her death." When Thanatos said the word, I felt my heart sink. I wondered how I could still feel at this point.

Zeus seemingly ignored him, directing his full attention on me now. He wrapped an arm around my back and led me a few steps away from Thanatos so he couldn't hear what he was about to say. His skin was warm against mine and made me feel like I had come back to life again somehow.

"Thanatos will walk you to your death, but do not be fearful, for you will come back in a new form. In your truest of forms. He must not know this as he must carry out his duty as the god of death, for if he cannot do that, he must be banished anyway. You will go with him and we will see one another again, I assure you."

The questions flooded my mind, but I couldn't figure out what I could possibly ask that was of most importance in comparison to everything else. I nodded as if I understood what he was saying, even though I couldn't comprehend a single word. When I turned away from Zeus and back toward Thanatos, the last strike of lightning came and announced his exit.

356

I ran to Thanatos and clung to him as tight as I could. He seemed repulsed by my touch, and I backed my head away, confused.

"What?" I asked, cocking my head to the side.

"I wish we had more time."

"But why did you back up when I tried to hug you?"

"When you touched me, you started the process. Now, as soon as I let go of you, you will be gone. I am just a guide."

"You said yourself that you will see me again someday," I reassured him, not wanting to give away anything Zeus had told me. It broke my heart to keep anything from him, especially when I knew it would help.

"I just can't keep losing you. This keeps happening again and again."

I grabbed his chin in my hand and lifted his head up to look at me. His ocean blue eyes were red with both rage and hurt.

"Remember," I said, pressing my palm to his heart just as he did to me. "I am here, always."

The corner of his mouth lifted into a slight smile, and his lips met mine. As soon as I drew back from him, the darkness that surrounded was now gone and all that remained was light. All around me was nothing but a blank canvas that must have matched the very beginning of time. No other soul existed near me; it was just me and the light. Nothing else. No one else. I looked down at the clothes I wore and the olive jacket was gone. In its place was a white robe that blended in with my surroundings. Just a few feet away, there was a small speck of gray that stood out amongst the white.

As I crept towards it, it became more clear exactly what it was. The final piece to the puzzle: the key.

LAND OF LIGHT

34

I looked all around, pacing and pacing in this land of light to find a keyhole, but no matter where I turned, there was nothing. I finally sat down, aggravated at myself and everything else that my life had become. The constant chase to solve cases and bring peace to the world turned into nothing but an unending game. A game you could never win. Looking back on my life, I realized how much I tried to help and be there for others when the last person I helped each day was myself. But how could a flower bloom and give pollen when it wasn't watered to begin with? Eventually, I would have met my breaking point. I lay back, camouflaging myself with the white surroundings. This place was so vast that I saw no end in sight. It was overwhelming and lonely. I played with the key in my hands and rubbed my fingertips along the ridges. It was different from the one that I had used to escape each time that I did. Izzy likely still had the old one. The one I now held had gold ridges along it and leaf embellishments wrapped around the sides. It reminded me of the gate to Olympus.

There was a sudden magnetic pull toward my chest. I gave in to it and the key pierced through the place that Thanatos had pressed his palm against. There was surprisingly no pain at all. I looked down at the key that stuck out of my chest and winced as I turned it, expecting to feel pain like a knife straight through me.

There was none. With a single turn of the key, it disappeared from sight and I was now on the cloud past the gate of Mount Olympus. The key had somehow brought me past the gate that was so carefully guarded. When I looked behind me, I saw Zeus sitting on his throne, smiling proudly.

"It took you long enough," he chuckled, each laugh bellowing out like thunder.

"Well gee, you could have said there would be a key I had to insert into my chest. That little detail was left out." I crossed my arms over my chest. The new wardrobe I was given would definitely not fit in anywhere else. I waited for a few moments to see if he was going to explain what was going on.

"Alice, you have proven your life in the human kingdom and it has been spared. The light you have not only shown to your kind but also ours, is something that would have been deemed impossible." He stood up and began walking toward me. "This is not something that happens easily, but I feel you have shown me humans can be more than I once thought they were. Although your death came at a time we least expected, you are now here in your new form, a goddess of Mount Olympus."

"What?!" was all I could manage to say.

When he got just a few steps away from me, I felt something extend from my shoulders. I looked left and right, seeing white wings extend on each side of me. They contrasted with Thanatos's black wings. It spooked me and I nearly jumped, but had nowhere to run. I felt like I was about to have a nervous breakdown when Zeus reached out for my hand and the warmth of his touch calmed me down. He pulled out one hand from behind him and pushed an object into my hand.

I picked it up, realizing it was an orb of light. I was afraid it would fall from my grasp, but no matter where I tilted my hand, it remained there. When I closed my hand to a fist and reopened it, the orb stayed unaffected.

"You are light. When you see the darkness, you will be able to show them the light they need in order to keep going, whether they be human or god. This is your calling," he said.

"But isn't Thanatos darkness?" I couldn't help but ask. He smiled and roaring laughter came from him.

"And isn't that so true? The light is attracted to darkness as darkness is attracted to the light. Together, both of you are whole. Apart, one will always yearn for the other."

"Oh no. He thinks I am gone. I need to tell him," I said. "Is he here?"

"You will find him where your heart learned to love."

The cryptic messages that Zeus gave didn't help very much. When I went to shake his hand, he shook his head and enveloped me in a hug, nearly breaking me like a toothpick. If I was still in human form, I would have likely died from his powerful embrace. I walked past the other gods and goddesses in a hurry, not even stopping to introduce myself or say hi. When I got to the edge of the cloud, I looked down before me and paced back and forth, not knowing if I could fully trust my wings. After debating for what felt like a while, I felt a push from behind me and I fell off the cloud. My wings shot out and acted as a parachute. I controlled them so I was able to come back up to see who had pushed me and found Heracles at the edge of the cloud where I had just stood.

"First you kill me, then you try again?" I asked.

"Oh, come on. I did you a favor," he said. I was surprised he wasn't even going to apologize. If he hadn't killed me, even though it was accidental, I would have never become a goddess. I would never admit it, though. Not in front of him, anyway. "What are you waiting for? Go find him!"

I turned around and let my wings guide me back down to earth. Lower and lower, I could see the church where I was brutally beaten and then saved by Thanatos. I went by the abandoned library where we first made love and I learned of his past. By the station where I first set my eyes on him. All these places made the memories rush back in, but I knew none of them were where my heart learned to love. I kept going past my townhome, where Toulouse was probably worried sick. I hoped Izzy went back there to at least take care of him. At least they were worried sick together instead of alone.

As I passed all the places I frequented in my human life, it became much more clear to me where I needed to go. I arrived at my parents' house and saw father kneeling down on the pavement with his head in his hands. Mother was at his side, rubbing his back. Thanatos stood before both of them; he was the one who likely bore the news to them. It showed me he was the complete opposite of a coward. Anyone else wouldn't have wanted the confrontation of telling a father and mother that their only child was gone. It would've been more painful to bear the truth to them as opposed to concealing it and letting them at least retain their hope. But it was a necessary thing.

I swooped down before them and somehow landed on my feet. The only thing was that I hadn't exactly figured out how to hide my wings. I would have to explain this along with everything else, too.

"Mom, Dad..." I began, and they lifted their heads. Mom was the first to rub her eyes, as if she couldn't believe what she saw before her.

"Look! Look! Maybe our lives are over too. Look who's in front of us!" she said. Silly mom.

"I don't know. Can you die from crying too much?" Dad said. He was the most sensitive man I have ever known and being with Thanatos had reminded me of him in that positive aspect.

"Come on, look!" she repeated. Thanatos had already turned and looked stunned, but he stayed exactly where he stood. When Dad looked up, he rushed over to me and hugged me, not even questioning the wings at first.

"Oh, Alice. I thought you were gone. Thanatos said you had been in an accident. My life was over, thinking you were gone. Don't scare me like that again. Please, please, please," he said.

"Dad, I'm okay. We're okay. Everything's okay."

Mom came over to give me a hug and I could see the tears coming from her eyes, except this time they were tears of happiness. "Okay, okay. Give her some space."

Dad clearly refused as he clung on to me.

"Let's go inside so that she can tell us what happened," she said. Dad nodded his head, but was holding me like I was his own personal teddy bear and clung to my side on the way into the house. Thanatos followed closely behind.

"So, would you like to begin by explaining the wings?" she asked, and we all laughed as I had now figured out how to retract them so I could make it through the front door.

"I guess that's a start."

LIGHT &
DARKNESS

35

"Wait a minute. Wait a minute... You mean to tell me you jumped in front of a god who was wielding a bat that had thorns poking out of it?!" Dad asked, clearly taken aback.

"Hey you can't yell at me for that. You're the one who raised me to protect others," I said.

"But yourself first!" he argued back.

"When do you put yourself first, Dad? Hmm?" I asked, knowing the answer already. He grunted and crossed his arms. It was not often I won an argument, but I knew that was one I could remember for a while.

"Zeus would never do something like this. I had no idea. When I was walking you to your death…did you know about this the whole time?" Thanatos asked.

I was hoping to avoid that question, but it looked like I now had to face it instead.

"Yes…but he said I had to keep it from you."

"Okay, wait. I am still trying to process the whole idea of there being gods and goddesses and YOU HAVE WINGS!" Mother was still back at the beginning of the conversation we were all having.

"I'm still trying to process it too and I don't think I'll ever be done trying to figure it out," I admitted.

"So then you can't die? So I don't have to worry about something ever happening to you then? God, this is the best day ever!" Dad shouted. He ran into the kitchen to go make exactly what I knew he was about to make. A big bowl of yellow cake batter he wouldn't put in the oven only so he could stick it in the fridge and eat spoonfuls of. It was also a miracle he was still here, too, with all that raw egg he had ingested over time. I laughed to myself.

"Okay. We need to have a big celebration," Mom said. She loved having get togethers and would find an excuse out of anything to do so.

"Who will be at this so-called celebration when the entire town hates me?" I asked.

"Oh, nonsense. They probably hate themselves more," she said. Thanatos and I both laughed.

"Hey umm, is it okay if I take Alice out for a little while?" Thanatos asked, to my surprise.

"Just don't lose her. She's hard to find, but very easy to lose," Dad said, stirring the bowl of cake batter and getting ready to eat a nice heaping spoonful.

Thanatos took my hand, and we walked out the back door into the woods. "So I can't help but to see a bit of a problem," he said.

"Yeah, what's that?" I asked.

"You are the complete opposite of me."

"And that's a problem, how?"

"Wouldn't you be more fitting with someone who was your type?" he asked. It was surprising to see this side of him. He was usually one to think more highly of himself.

"Each puzzle piece needs its opposite in order to fit into the bigger picture of the world. And now I know I have finally found mine," I admitted. He took my hands in his and we both went up into the sky, nearing Mount Olympus. The pink and orange hues of the sunset surrounded us. When I looked at him, I knew I could live forever in his heart.

"That couldn't have been said more perfectly."

"Why thank you, I guess I'm getting a hang of this being a goddess thing already."

"I have to admit it was my fault Hypnos found you out," he said.

"What do you mean?"

"I was planning something really big, and it was too difficult to hide from him, especially being my brother and all. It made him even more angry to see, and that's why he wanted to torture you more than me."

"What was it?"

Without answering, Thanatos dropped to his knee, floating in the sky before me as if there were an invisible floor beneath us. He pulled out an emerald and diamond ring that had been embellished with gold leaves all around it from his pocket. His hand shakily took mine in his and before placing the ring on my finger, he looked up into my eyes.

"Alice, goddess or not, you have shown me a light in this world that I never thought I would find. Fate continues to bring you back into my life again and again, like a magnetic force that can't be controlled. And even if I could, I wouldn't. No time with you would be enough, but any amount of time wouldn't go unappreciated. You are like no one I have ever met before and have a way of washing out any doubts I ever felt.

"Alice, I can't imagine a life without you, nor do I want to. No matter what problems happen, I want to be by your side through the whole thing. And I promise you I will always try to be the best that I can for you. In my time here on Earth, I've seen humans have this tradition. So...will you marry me?"

I put both my hands over my mouth as my jaw dropped. There was only one answer I had in mind; I just had to find my voice.

"You *are* the best you can be. You don't have to change. Yes, yes, yes! Absolutely, yes!" I screamed, and allowed him to place the ring on my finger. I hugged him so tight and as our wings wrapped around one another, light met darkness in the most fulfilling embrace that two opposites could have possibly encountered.

ACKNOWLEDGEMENTS

Thank you to those that I have lost for always sending reminders even when you are no longer here physically. I couldn't have done this without you.

I am grateful for the Maryland Writing Association for providing countless workshops and networking opportunities to learn more about publishing and writing.

Thank you to my family and friends for supporting me on my writing journey and always cheering me on. I couldn't do it without you!

ABOUT THE AUTHOR

Marissa is the author of a memoir and the Tales of Charles Island series. Marissa mostly writes fictional stories and began by journaling and writing screenplays in elementary school. She spends much of her time with her pets aside from traveling to new places and teaching. Born and raised in Connecticut, she holds New England close to her heart and many of her stories are based in the suburbs of New England.

She has a deep and profound respect for people with special needs as her first job in her field was a special educator. Marissa found her voice through writing. While in high school, she was the editor of the Arts and Entertainment section of the school newspaper. She pursued a degree in Education, minoring in English literature and Anthropology. Later, she went back to school to better understand Autism and graduated with a Master's in Special Education.

Marissa would love to hear from you. Use the links below to connect & hear about upcoming books:

Visit Marissa's Website:

www.mystywrites.com

Instagram:

www.instagram.com/_mysty_writes/

Amazon Page:

www.amazon.com/author/marissadangelo

Made in the USA
Middletown, DE
16 June 2023

32745524R00215